MOON OVER MAALAEA BAY

H. L. Wegley

MOON OVER MAALAEA BAY

Contact Information: titleadmin@pelicanbookgroup.com

Scripture quotations, unless otherwise indicated are taken from the King James translation, public domain.

Cover Art by *Nicola Martinez*

Harbourlight Books, a division of Pelican Ventures, LLC
www.pelicanbookgroup.com PO Box 1738 *Aztec, NM * 87410

Harbourlight Books sail and mast logo is a trademark of Pelican Ventures, LLC

Publishing History
First Harbourlight Edition, 2014
Paperback Edition ISBN 978-1-61116-325-4
Electronic Edition ISBN 978-1-61116-324-7
Published in the United States of America

Dedication

This book is dedicated to my cousin, Mary, who remained joyful and encouraged others despite a long, crippling disease. She knew that her Lord is Elohim-Yachal, the God of Hope, the One she could trust. Shortly before this book was contracted, Mary graduated to heaven where she now runs free like the young girl I remember as a child.

Praise for H.L. Wegley

Hide and Seek

"The author has done a great job of weaving a very exciting, well written story together that I could not put down until I finished it in one reading. I had to find out what happened." ~ Thomas H. Hinke, IT/Computing Security

"Mr. Wegley—let's see more of Jennifer & Lee. Either write faster, or get your publisher to publish faster. I'm waiting!" ~ Kate Hinke, Writer & Editor

"...the story really comes alive and pulls you along for a heart-stopping ride. *Hide and Seek* by H.L. Wegley is a definite keeper if you love suspense with a touch of romance. " ~ Ginger Solomon

1

In light of recent events, she should be dead. Jennifer Akihara should no longer exist.

And now she doesn't.

The thought brought a smile to her lips.

Nearly nine hours ago, in another world three thousand miles away, Jennifer Akihara became Mrs. Lee Brandt. "Jennifer Brandt," she whispered. It sounded right. It *was* right. And the dangers that nearly prevented her from taking Lee's name were gone, either locked away in a federal prison or dead.

Spending her wedding night with Lee in a tropical paradise would be the perfect start to their life as man and wife. But the perfect start had been delayed.

In the fading twilight, under a purple sky, Jennifer glanced up at Lee's brilliant, blue eyes as he walked beside her in his cargo shorts and muscle shirt, looking—she hated clichés, but there was simply no other word for him—hot. Tonight, on this island, extremely hot. And the warm, humid trade winds, which caressed her skin and ruffled Lee's hair, cooled nothing.

Lee seemed unusually quiet. Maybe he was disappointed about their room not being ready.

She moved close to him, gently brushing against his side with each step as they strolled through the menagerie of colorful Kihei shops. The fragrance of pineapple, mango, and coconut mingled with those of cloves and cinnamon near the kiosks selling soaps, candles, and lotions.

She looked up at him, wondering what was on his mind. It was time to probe. "If someone hadn't broken into our room just before we arrived, right now we would be—"

"We'd be watching the moon over Maalaea Bay out that big window. I know."

"If *someone* hadn't insisted on *that* room, maybe we could've gotten *another* room, and we could be—"

"I know, sweetheart. But when you see the sunset from our room tomorrow evening, you'll understand. That room is special. We can eat dinner here at the shops, and by 7:30 our room door will be fixed and the electronics that were stolen will all be replaced, just like the manager promised. And…we get a free night for our inconvenience."

"Inconvenience? That's hardly the word for what I feel." She met his gaze with love and longing in her eyes.

Thoughts of being alone with him filled her mind. She touched her face. Like Lee, it was hot.

He smiled at her. "You should see your cheeks, Jenn."

Her hand jerked back to her face.

"Didn't you overdo the blush a little?" He looked down at her and grinned.

His grin told her he was back from wherever his mind had wondered, and he knew exactly what she was thinking. Lee was an expert at reading her mind, and he loved to tease her, especially when the teasing turned her permanently tan cheeks a rosy red.

"In this climate a woman doesn't need makeup to—" Her cell phone filled the tropical night with the spirited sounds of "The Texas Aggie War Hymn."

"Lee!" She stared into his laughing eyes, vacillating between jabbing him in the ribs and kissing his smiling lips. "I can't believe you talked me into loading that ring tone on my phone."

"Too bad I only get to hear it when the caller ID's blocked. Bet it's Peterson. Calls from his FBI phone are always blocked. Aren't you going to answer it?"

"Only *this* call. Then I'm turning this insidious little device, with your alma mater's fight song on it, *off*." She stopped, flipped her cell open, and raised it to her ear. "This is Jennifer Aki—I mean Jennifer Brandt...No, we're fine. Don't concern yourself, and please stop calling." Her voice rose, but the heat of her anger quickly dropped in temperature to an icy chill.

She snapped the phone shut and stood staring across the shops into the dark parking lot beyond. Who was he? Was she being stalked again? No. It couldn't—

"What was that about? We're on our honeymoon. It's our wedding night. Peterson wouldn't actually—"

"It wasn't Peterson." She shivered. The warm, Maui evening had grown cold. The trade winds became an arctic blast. She put her arms around Lee and pressed her cheek into his chest. The two phone calls and the incident with the room were upsetting. "It was the same man who called while we were at SeaTac. Still asking questions. Still claiming to be Peterson's assistant, but—"

"But Peterson hasn't had an assistant since Bastian washed out of the bureau."

She looked up at him.

He studied her face, and his winning smile returned. "Don't let it upset you, sweetheart. You're still a celebrity in Seattle, especially after rescuing Katie and the other girls from the traffickers. The media can't get enough of you. They're probably trying to spy on you during our honeymoon. You've got paparazzi problems." He scanned her slowly, systematically. "I can't say that I blame them, especially when you hit the beach in your swimsuit tomorrow." He slipped his arms around her. "We'll keep a low profile on the island. I won't let them bother us."

After hearing his voice, his reassuring words, and now feeling his arms around her, Jennifer's chill warmed to a more comfortable temperature. "You're probably right." She pressed the power button on her cell. It played its farewell tune as she dropped it into her shorts pocket. "Well, they can't call anymore." She sighed and clasped her hands behind Lee's neck, letting the love in his eyes pull her to a place she wanted to remain forever. "Now where were we?"

He pulled her close.

She didn't resist. There was no reason to resist. Not now. Not ever again. As she had vowed a few hours ago, from this day forward she was his completely. When their lips met, the night grew warm again. But Lee's kiss was several degrees hotter than warm, promising much, much more.

"Where we were, was on our way to dinner. Then back to our room."

"What time is it?"

"It's almost 7:00."

She cupped his cheek with her hand. "I've got a proposition for you, Mr. Brandt. Our room is almost ready, so let's skip dinner, get a couple of iced lattes, and drink them on the way back to our room. We only stood on the balcony for a few minutes, but I know that right now, waves are splashing just underneath the bedroom window. Look." She pointed into the western sky. "The moon's nearly full over Maalaea Bay. It'll be shining in through the big window and—"

He pressed a finger against her lips. "Shhh. It's a deal. You can be very persuasive when you want to be. Maybe you should've gone to law school instead of taking the research position with NSA." He gave her his coy smile. "Then again, making a proposal like that in a courtroom could get you disbarred."

She sought a witty reply, but her eyes caught a familiar image shining golden yellow inside the glass counter behind Lee. "Look. Gold whales tails. I lost mine the night of my master's ceremony." She refocused her gaze on Lee's eyes. "You could really ingratiate yourself with your bride by replacing it for her on her wedding night."

He rested his strong hands on her bare shoulders. At his touch, the night grew even warmer.

She stepped closer, pressing her cheek into his chest and listening to the rhythm of his heartbeat, her soul's favorite music.

"How grateful would Mrs. Brandt be?" He kissed her forehead.

She looked up and met his gaze. "More grateful than she's ever been. But first you need to walk to the espresso stand by the street and buy her an iced latte while she picks out a necklace."

"OK. Find your necklace." Lee's index finger traced a circle around her neck, then traced a path up to her chin, continuing until it touched the tip of her nose. "I'll be right back with our coffee." He strode away towards the espresso stand.

Jennifer's gaze returned to the jewelry counter where she searched for a whale-tail necklace like the one she had lost more than a year ago. Her search was soon forgotten when she became lost in anticipation of their time alone together and warm thoughts of her love for the man who had saved her life so many times in so many ways—the man who had introduced her to the one true God Who had saved her soul for eternity.

****

Lee walked down a long aisle between shops. Nearly halfway to the street, he stopped and turned to look at Jennifer.

Her hands rested lightly on the glass counter and her brown, almond-shaped eyes roved over the array of jewelry behind the glass. The trade winds blew gently through the shopping area animating the gentle waves in her dark hair, while the permanent tan from her Japanese-Hawaiian heritage created a stunning contrast to her white shorts and red tank top.

In his thirty years on the planet, Lee had never seen anyone as beautiful as Jennifer, a beauty that went deep, all the way to her heart.

Nine months ago he had given up searching for someone to spend his life with. He'd given up on his job. He had just given up, a man simply going through the motions of living. Then God used his mentor Howie and a terrorist conspiracy to bring them together. When God did things, He did them right.

Was it a match made in heaven? Yes. But due to the terrorists, it had started out in...well, the other place. Since that day, his life hadn't been the same. How could it be? He had fallen in love with a twenty-six-year-old Miss Universe who had an IQ rivaling Einstein's?

You fool. It's your wedding night. Stop gawking at her from forty feet away. Get the coffee, buy the necklace, and take her home. The moon isn't going to hang over Maalaea Bay forever.

He took one more longing look, mustered the strength to pull his gaze away from Jennifer's shapely form, and hurried towards the espresso stand.

Unlike the nearly deserted back row of shops where Jennifer waited for him, the sidewalk along South Kihei Road was filled with tourists enjoying the warm evening. The aroma of freshly ground Kona coffee could almost create a caffeine buzz simply by inhaling it.

Lee ordered two iced lattes. While he waited, he looked westward, above the gently swaying palm trees lining the beach. The moon was full, a bright silver disk in the western sky. Unlike the light pollution of Seattle, the lights of Kihei did little to dim the twinkling stars sprinkled generously across a field of dark-purple.

By the time the barista handed him the two icy drinks, he felt an ache deep inside. Lee smiled, realizing he already missed Jennifer. This was the longest time they'd been apart since they left for SeaTac Airport after their wedding ceremony. What would it be like if they ever had to endure a long separation?

He hurried down the aisle between the shops towards the back row where Jennifer hopefully had found her necklace.

Lee didn't see her as he approached the jewelry shop. She must have moved to the opposite counter.

A brightly clad Hawaiian lady now stood behind the counter, straightening her wares on the shelf above.

Good. They could purchase the necklace and then—he stopped. Jennifer wasn't at the opposite counter. Apprehension began incubating in his heart. He stepped to the display counter and tried to shut off the incubator. "Excuse me, ma'am. Did my wife find a necklace here?"

"Your wife? Since I returned from my break I haven't seen anyone." She shrugged and shook her head.

His apprehension now transcended incubation. "She was just here. About five foot two, long, dark hair, very beautiful."

The lady gave a frown. "No, I haven't seen—"

A commotion three shops away interrupted their conversation. A wide-eyed woman scurried towards the street, clutching her cell phone.

When he didn't see Jennifer there, he turned his attention back to the shopkeeper. "If she returns, tell her to wait for me. I'll be back in a minute."

"Check the ladies' room. When women disappear, nine times out of ten that's where they are."

"Thanks. I'll keep that in mind." He turned to search another row of shops, realizing his heart had shifted into a higher gear.

Lee wove back and forth through several adjacent rows, then looked down several perpendicular rows of shops. A nagging worry again tried to intrude. He squelched it.

He would check the ladies' room next. *Until I've done that, I'm not going to worry.*

He noticed a sign directing shoppers to the restrooms. He followed it.

A middle-aged lady with a pleasant smile approached.

He pulled out his wallet. "Excuse me, ma'am."

"Yes?"

"I seem to have misplaced my wife. While you're inside, would you mind checking to see if she's there? Her name is Jennifer." He slipped their engagement picture from his wallet and held it out for her to see. "Here's her picture."

The woman's eyes immediately focused on his ring, then her gaze went to the picture. A wise woman. "Sure, I'll see if—my, she's a real beauty. I'll let you know when I leave, or I'll send Jennifer out to you."

"Thanks, ma'am."

As the lady entered the building, the wail of a distant siren grew louder. It was joined by several other sirens. The knot forming in his stomach tightened. When the sirens converged on the side of the shops bordering South Kihei Road, he felt a strong urge to run towards the flashing red and blue lights. But he needed to wait for the lady. He might be worried about nothing.

What's taking her so long?

The door opened, and the lady walked towards him, now frowning. "Your wife isn't in there, and no one inside remembers seeing her."

"Ma'am, are you absolutely sure?"

"Yes. I'm sorry, but she's not there."

"Thanks."

A sinking sensation sent his stomach into a nauseating freefall. His rising panic drummed in his chest. Lee whirled towards the flashing lights along the street and trotted in that direction.

Three police cars had parked hurriedly in disarray near the curb. A small crowd of people gathered near them. The buzz of their conversation was too far away to understand any of it.

While Lee jogged towards the street, he passed an open-air sports bar, where a large, flat-screen TV flashed a bright red message. People crowded around it, excitement mixed with concern on their faces.

Lee stopped when he saw the two large words, "Amber Alert." Another message scrolled across the screen. He maneuvered between two taller men to read it. "Teenage girl abducted from Kihei shops at 7:00 PM. Description Asian, five foot one to five foot three, sixteen or seventeen years old, last seen wearing a red tank top and white shorts.

It was Jennifer's description on the screen. Being petite, she could have easily been mistaken for a younger person. He glanced at his watch. 7:15 PM. She had disappeared at 7:00 PM. With his heart pounding out the tempo of terror, Lee sprinted towards the ominous lights of the police cars.

2

Lee ran towards two policemen engaged in conversation beside the nearest patrol car. As he approached, they spun to him, their hands simultaneously reaching for their guns.

He stopped, shoved his palms towards them, and yelled between breaths. "The kidnapped girl!"

The tall officer had drawn his weapon, but kept it pointing downward.

The shorter policeman met his gaze and studied his face. "Do you have some information about her?"

"Yeah. She's not a girl. She's my wife, Jennifer Akihara, now Jennifer Brandt. We're here on our honeymoon. One second she was here, then she was gone."

"And you are?" The taller officer said, holstering his gun.

"Lee Brandt." His trembling fingers struggled to pull out his wallet. He took one agonizing look at the photo then handed them the wallet-sized, engagement picture. "Here's a picture of her."

The two officers studied it for a moment.

"Matches the description we got," the shorter one said.

"I'll say it does, but not many women can match her." The taller officer pursed his lips as he turned towards Lee. "Let me give you some advice. It's not a good idea to run up to officers here like you're going to attack them. There's Maile Amber Alert; we're in the process of locking down this entire area." He paused. "Now, can you tell us anything else about her disappearance?"

What had been circulating on the periphery of Lee's conscious mind suddenly became an intuitive conclusion. Whatever the consequences, he decided to go with it. "Officer, this isn't a random abduction. And she's an adult. She's twenty-six."

The shorter officer flashed him a glance. There was sympathy in it. The first encouraging thing he had noticed in the last half hour.

"I'm Officer Yagi, Mr. Brandt." He stuck out a thumb at the taller guy beside him. "This is Officer Kaai. What makes you think this was a targeted attack?"

Lee took a calming breath. How should he tell them this story? He just needed to state the bare facts. "Jennifer and I recently amputated one arm of an international sex-trafficking ring—a fifty-million-dollar-a-year arm. Somebody's unhappy about what—"

"Yagi, it's that babe, uh, lady from Seattle. This story broke a few weeks ago."

"I remember her. Who could forget?" Yagi looked at Lee and pointed to his patrol car. "We'll need you to come to the station with us. This case is going to get elevated in a hurry. I'll call in what you've told us and send the picture ahead while we're on the way. We will need to get the FBI invol—"

"Call the Seattle Field Office." Lee interrupted. "Agent Peterson there has been on the trafficking case from the beginning."

"I'll pass that on. But there are official channels we

need to use for notifying other agencies." Yagi opened the back door of the patrol car and gestured towards it.

"Fine." *I'll use my own channel.* Lee pulled out his cell and climbed into the back seat, a cage that felt like a prison. Being locked into the confined space was getting to him. He needed air and used his call to keep his mind off the rising panic.

With Kaai driving, Yagi's words flowed in a long, steady stream as he passed information to the local police.

Lee hit Peterson's FBI cell number on his speed dial, placing a call the agent would answer if at all possible. There was a long delay while the call went through to the mainland. The delay was followed by several rings.

Come on, Peterson, answer.

"Agent Peterson here."

Lee looked out the window and up into the night sky. *Thanks.*

"Peterson, Lee Brandt. Someone abducted Jennifer here on Maui and—"

"What!" Peterson boomed out, followed by a rare expletive. "You two are on your honeymoon. Who would…"

"It's got to be an international component of the trafficking ring. I think they're trying to make Jennifer an example. But someone here thought she was a teenager, so there's an Amber Alert out for her."

"That's a good thing. Using the alert, I can lock down the whole island. All of the islands if I have to. Where are you now, Lee."

"In a patrol car on the way to the police station in Wailuku."

"Good. Tell them everything you know and even

what you only suspect. We need to get every law-enforcement wheel turning. I have to go now, so I can notify the appropriate people. If this plays out like I believe it will, you might see me very soon. Whatever it takes, we'll get Jennifer back."

"Thanks, Peterson." Lee closed his cell. Peterson might come. Lee prayed he would.

Officer Kaai's eyes were staring at him in the rearview mirror. "Who were you talking to, Brandt?"

He stared back at the shadowy face in the mirror. "Agent Peterson, FBI in Seattle. The guy I told you about."

Kaai dipped his head. "Guess it can't hurt. I'm just not used to seeing people make cell calls from the back of my patrol car. Makes me a little nervous."

Lee looked at the reflection of the officer's eyes in the rearview mirror. "If I know Peterson, he's about to make all of us a little nervous."

A few glimmers of hope had been tossed to him, but the darkness of his circumstances sent Lee to a place he couldn't bear to visit. He fought against the pictures invading his mind, but he relived those moments when he had nearly lost Jennifer six weeks ago. Though he was sure he'd lost her, God had rescued Jennifer, and He had used Lee to help in her rescue. In less than two hours, he had gone from the depths of despair to elation. Would that happen again? Could he be as fortunate a second time?

Reality set in. These were wealthy, international criminals. Their attack had obviously been well planned. Someone had closely watched Jennifer and him. The abductors had chosen their time carefully and grabbed her at an opportune moment. These facts alone told him the odds were long that he'd ever see

Jennifer alive.

As despair set in, he held onto one hope. Jennifer was twenty-six years old, so the traffickers hadn't planned for an Amber Alert. At least one monkey wrench had been thrown into their plan. But would it be enough to save Jennifer?

3

While the patrol car rolled across the island towards Wailuku, Lee tried praying, but questions interfered—a myriad of questions. However, they all led to the same one. Why?

The knots in his writhing stomach and his panic brought on nausea. Soon, fighting the urge to vomit also interfered with each attempt to pray. And then the questions returned.

Why on their wedding night? Why did God allow it? Jennifer was so brilliant, so beautiful, so full of compassion for lost and oppressed people...why her?

Dark fields gave way to dark, shadowy palm trees. Soon scattered lights appeared on the hill to the left, and the lights of the city lay only a short distance ahead. A few more minutes and he—a thought jarred him. How could he have forgotten to ask?

You're an idiot, Brandt! An INTJ idiot. *The Meyers-Briggs personality assessment made him understand himself a lot better. It sometimes even led to an intuitive, brilliant leap of logic.*

He leaned forward. "Officer Yagi."

Yagi twisted in his seat. "Yeah, Brandt?"

"An Amber Alert means there was a witness. Who saw the abduction? What did they see?"

Yagi looked at Kaai and waited.

After a few seconds Kaai nodded.

Yagi turned back towards Lee. "A tourist, a

middle-aged lady, saw two men overpower and abduct your wife." Yagi sighed. "It happened at the back of the shops. They came out of the dark parking area in the rear of the shops, grabbed her, and left the same way, into the dark parking lot."

"Anything else? Any other witnesses?"

Yagi shook his head. "No. Just one lady saw it."

Jennifer would have fought them. She was fast, smart, and she knew some karate. Why didn't they mention that? "What about descriptions of the two perps?"

"Perps?" Yagi glanced his way and shook his head. "You watch too much TV."

"I seldom watch TV, Yagi. Now tell me about the perps!" Lee's frustrated voice surprised even him with its intensity.

"Settle down, man. I was getting there. Two strongly built men wearing dark clothing. That's all we have to go on." Yagi turned back towards the windshield. He was done.

But there had to be more. Lee wasn't ready to quit his interrogation. "What kind of dark clothes? Shorts? T-shirts?"

"The lady was so upset by—" Yagi cut off his sentence and paused.

What was he about to say?

"It upset the lady so much that's all she could give us for a description. Now, the police station is a couple of blocks ahead. You can expect a lot of questions, Brandt. If we're going to help you, you're going to have to give us everything you know about Jennifer, a complete core dump."

Unlike the core dump you just truncated.

Yagi had omitted something that further upset the

lady. Lee would find out what it was…somehow. The little things that seemed to be missing bothered him. Was there more to Jennifer's abduction than he suspected? His gut said yes. His gut also said he should vomit. He tried to ignore his gut…on both counts.

Lee sighed. "Core dump. You must be into computers."

Yagi nodded, then shrugged. "But that was before I got hooked on law enforcement."

Kaai turned into a parking area adjacent to a building that appeared to be a beehive of activity.

"Here we are," Yagi announced. "Brace yourself, Brandt."

****

An hour later, Lee sat alone in the room where he had faced a fever-pitched interrogation for forty-five minutes. Detective Ramirez of the Maui Police Department, MPD, was good and thorough. He'd asked Lee a lot of questions, but only allowed him a few in return. He understood. Ramirez was probably under intense pressure from the politicians. Tourism could be severely—

His cell rang. The number was blocked. Lee answered.

"Is that you, Brandt?"

Peterson. He prayed for good news. "Yeah. Lee here. Have you—"

"Just listen for a second, because that's all I have. Some people in very high places are concerned about Jennifer falling into the wrong hands, and they're—"

"Peterson! She's in the wrong hands now!"

If the tall FBI agent were here, Lee would be in his face. He needed to be in somebody's face.

Peterson sighed. "I know. But hear me out. They're pulling out all of the stops. That's a good thing. In fact, I'll see you in about four and a half hours, so—"

"Four and a half hours? That's not possible. What—"

"Lee, I told you they're pulling out all the stops. Don't ask anymore because I can't tell you." Peterson paused. Someone in the background spoke. "Make that four hours. Sit tight and try not to worry. We'll find Jennifer." He ended the call.

The words "We'll find Jennifer" replayed in his mind. But the thought of how they might find her brought more nausea.

Was Peterson coming on something supersonic? A military plane? He said Uncle Sam was pulling out all the stops. But going to such lengths to get him on the ground in Maui meant that the FBI agent knew a lot more about this incident than he was telling.

The attention Jennifer was getting was comforting, the reasons behind it, disconcerting.

Lee's stomach roiled and he leaped from his seat, ran out the door, and headed towards a sign in the hallway that pointed to restrooms.

After five minutes of violent retching, his stomach settled. He washed his face, and then his mind cleared. Now a new thought dominated all others. With all of the pressure being brought to bear on them, her abductors couldn't move Jennifer. As the search continued, at some point they would probably kill her rather than risk being caught red-handed.

He tried to come up with a plan—*his* plan for

finding Jennifer. He would rather die trying to save her than sit idly by and let some goons kill her. The police wouldn't take kindly to his meddling, so he wouldn't tell them what he was doing. But he hadn't a clue yet what he was going to do.

Before he formulated his plan, Lee needed to make a phone call. It was a call to the man who had given Jennifer away to him earlier that day, a call to the man who trusted Lee to protect her, a call that filled him with dread.

4

Lee stood in the hallway outside the men's room in the Wailuku police station and pressed Granddad's number on his speed dial. He sought words to break the news. The right words wouldn't come, only feelings of horror and loss. That wasn't the message he wanted to communicate. He needed to give them some hope, but right now, hope was in short supply.

You can't give what you don't have.

"Hello."

Granddad's voice. He sounded cheerful. Probably having the time of his life with Katie, playing chess, throwing baseballs, and teaching her karate. It was all about to change.

Lee and Jennifer were in the process of adopting Katie. The paperwork was completed. But if something happened to Jennifer, what would happen to their plans? What would happen to Katie? It was too much to contemplate all at once. So much hung in the balance for the people he loved most.

"Hello. Is anyone there?"

"Granddad, it's Lee."

He had to wake up, stop letting his mind wander.

"Lee, you should be enjoying your honeymoon, not calling me. Katie and I are having a good time. She—"

"Granddad, I have bad news."

Silence.

He took a breath and related the facts of Jennifer's abduction, including the Amber Alert and Peterson's involvement. "The Amber Alert will help—"

"We killed all of them! How could they have taken Jenn?" Katie's voice. She must have picked up the other phone.

He sought a reply, a way to explain the unexplainable to a girl who worshiped the ground Jennifer walked on. "Katie, you told us a girl helped the traffickers when you were taken. She's never been apprehended, so there has to be more to this trafficking operation than we know about. When we killed Boatman's and Trader's cohorts, maybe we drew the anger of the international syndicate."

"We've got to find her." Katie's voice was full of determination. This strong, bright, and beautiful fifteen-year-old could not be deterred. At least he'd never been able to when she was on a crusade. She was a great girl, but keeping her out of danger would be a full-time proposition. He couldn't handle that and implement his own plan for—

"Did you hear me, Lee? I'm coming to help find Jenn. And you aren't—"

"We're both coming." Grandfather interjected in his trump-suit voice. "Katie, rest assured you *will* be coming with me, so please hang up the phone while I convince Lee of that."

A click sounded. Good. At least she respected Granddad's authority. Lee's first look at the small, fit, seventy-year-old man who held a sixth-degree black belt in karate had also commanded Lee's respect. But on this, he had to oppose Granddad.

"Now, Lee, you—"

"No. You can't endanger Katie. I won't let—"

"Please, Lee. Listen for a moment."

"OK. I'm listening." *But you're not gonna change my mind.*

"I don't believe it will, but if this turns out badly and you keep Katie from helping, do you realize what that would do to her? Katie and Jennifer are closer than most mothers and daughters even though the adoption hasn't been finalized. It would kill Katie if…"

Granddad was right.

Lee might keep Katie safe physically, but emotionally, it could destroy her. Maybe all this would be over even before they arrived. "OK. Katie comes on one condition, Granddad. She stays out of the line of fire."

"And who determines where the hooligans' guns are aimed?" Granddad asked.

Lee had never tried to assert his authority over Granddad. He was the authority figure in Jennifer's family. Not knowing what to expect, Lee replied, "I do."

Granddad sighed. "As you wish. I've got to go now, Lee. I have relatives on Maui to contact, and we've got to pack. We'll catch, what is it you call it, the red-eye? Katie and I will be there in about ten hours."

When he terminated the call, Lee had won one battle, but it felt like he had lost the war. Worry went viral in the neural network of his mind, worry about Katie, and worry about Jennifer. Both were brilliant, geniuses. But intelligence could only do so much against men with overpowering strength. Men full of evil, evil that knew no limits.

There was One Who was all-powerful, One full of love, grace, and mercy that knew no limits.

Lee closed his eyes and took his concerns to that

all-powerful source.

Footsteps grew louder, and he ended his prayer. A uniformed, male officer sauntered down the hallway towards him. The officer passed by Lee and entered the men's room.

Lee walked to Detective Ramirez's desk, reflecting on his personal plan to find Jennifer. Lee was unsure of his next move. But move he must, or the part of his sanity that remained would evaporate like a drop of water at noon in the Sahara.

To find Jennifer, he must first find her captors. The only source to tap for more information was the lone eyewitness to the abduction, the lady Yagi had mentioned. To find her he would need to find out where—

The scene near the detective's desk caught his attention. Ramirez was talking to a group of officers. Numerous papers and folders lay spread in disarray across his desk. It was an interesting development. What if...

He stopped on the opposite side of the desk. The detective, still engrossed in conversation, hadn't noticed him.

Lee scanned the papers on the desk looking for any morsel of helpful information. One paper caught his eye. Someone had scribbled Amber Alert in large letters. Below the two words were many words written in small letters.

He stepped closer and read, Grand Wailea Resort, Chapel Wing, Room 414. Below that was a name, Bertha Renner. He memorized the information, then walked to the room where the detective had questioned him.

Near the door, Lee stopped. A laser printer sat on

a table beside the door. Beside it lay an opened ream of paper. He slid a sheet of paper from the stack and folded it into fourths. After he slipped into the room, he wrote down the contact information for Bertha Renner.

Lee was certain of two things. First, the police would have thoroughly interrogated this witness, pumping from her everything she knew. Second, Yagi hadn't told him everything Bertha Renner had seen.

5

Under a circle of electric tiki lights, Franklin James sat at a table on the deck of his yacht anchored off Makena. He looked at the short, bald Asian man who sat across the table, a revolting man, but nevertheless one he needed...for a while longer.

James drummed his fingers on the table. "So, do we complete the deal or just kill her?"

Nguyen frowned. His eyes said he was calculating, slowly, the only way this man could calculate. "She almost single-handedly dismembered our business. We will lose fifty million dollars this year because of Jennifer Akihara, Mr. James. She must pay, but we must be paid also."

"One correction, Nguyen. It's Jennifer Brandt now. You were not supposed to let that happen." James watched as Nguyen's forehead wrinkled.

Nguyen sighed. "Too bad we couldn't have taken her before the wedding. Things got a little too hot in Seattle. But no harm done. We took her in Maui instead, right after she arrived. Given her worthless religion, she's still salable as unused merchandise." A smirk bent his lips. "Maybe her Christianity is worth something...to us."

His smirk sickened James, but he remained silent and allowed Nguyen to make his point.

"So, Mr. James, I think we should give the prince his million-dollar baby and people will learn not to interfere with our business. This will send a strong message."

James wondered about Lee Brandt. The man was a genius like the woman. He might give them trouble. "So what about the bridegroom?"

Nguyen laughed in staccato bursts of mirthless tones. "We will pay him appropriately, with torture. We let Mr. Brandt live. Then we leak false pictures onto the Internet, showing his bride in a brothel in Ranong. That will repay him for his role."

James thought through Nguyen's suggestion. There was a risk he refused to overlook. "Lee Brandt will come looking."

Nguyen released two long bursts of mock laughter. "Let him search every brothel in Thailand. The prince will have her in his compound in—"

"Silence!" The word exploded from James's mouth. His fist pounded the table. James lowered his voice to slightly more than a whisper. "You can trust no one with her whereabouts. Not even crew members on my yacht. If the prince thinks we betrayed him, he will kill us as surely as the sun rises."

Nguyen's bald brow wrinkled. "Then perhaps we should eliminate your entire crew."

James sneered at the idiot's suggestion. "I think you should just eliminate your loose talk. Or perhaps someone will loosen your tongue...completely."

Nguyen's hand jerked to his mouth then returned to the table. He swallowed hard. The temperature was only in the seventies, but perspiration beaded on his bald brow. "So...so how do we hand her to the prince and collect our fee?"

It was good to learn the secret fears of those one did business with. One could use the knowledge to manipulate them…or to pay them. James smiled. "We will slip her onto his catamaran south of Lahaina. The prince pays us, then she becomes his problem."

Then one day soon I pay you, Nguyen.

Nguyen's crooked smile remained. "I know that his Dash 8 is fueled and ready at Lahaina Airport. Lee Brandt's precious million-dollar bride will soon be sold to a man who collects the most beautiful women in the world for his perverse entertainment." Nguyen smirked. "After he's finished with her, she won't be fit for Amsterdam or Manila. He will probably dump her in Calcutta, collect some pocket change, and she will die there unknown and unrecognizable."

Everything about the man sickened James. But he must tolerate this fool for a while longer if he wanted to attain a ten-digit income next year. At the appropriate time, he would relieve Nguyen of his duties…and his life.

The bald man's smirk grew into a smile. "Should we let her know what the prince will do to her? I would like to see her reaction. It would ease our pain to watch hers."

"No, Nguyen. Trader underestimated her and Trader is dead. Let's not make her too desperate too soon. It would be a shame if she forced us to kill her. We should let her wait patiently for an opportunity to escape—one that will never come—until we have our money and she becomes the prince's problem." His fingers tapped an anapestic rhythm on the table. "It would not be wise to try to torture her now with stories of the torture she will soon experience."

****

Jennifer tried to snuggle closer to Lee, but he was so muscular, and he hadn't shaved. Were they lying down? No, they wouldn't do that...not yet. Her fuzzy thoughts swirled like cream stirred into her coffee until she could no longer distinguish one from the other.

Lee became a hard floor, and her warm thoughts of him suddenly morphed into their antithesis. *This is only a nightmare.* But it felt like one she'd had before.

She opened her eyes and all five senses sounded alarms. She tried to gasp. She couldn't. Tape covered her mouth. Her wrists were bound behind her. She'd felt like this before. But when? She tried to concentrate. Clarity eluded her. What had happened?

Slowly the fog dissipated. She felt this way after Trader drugged her.

So, I've been drugged.

What happened before that? She tried to concentrate, to remember.

She stood at the jewelry counter at the back of the Kihei shops. Beyond the light of the jewelry shop was the darkness of the unlit parking area. In the periphery of her vision, three shadowy figures emerged from that darkness, grabbing her before she recognized the danger. A hand clamped over her mouth and pulled her into the dark parking lot. An arm bent around her neck squeezing so tightly...she must've blacked out. It was the sleeper hold.

That's how Katie described her abduction by Trader. The sleeper hold and then drugs.

But Trader is dead.

If there was a connection to Katie's abduction, it must be from higher up, maybe from an international organization. But why would they—

An answer came to mind. It was the only one that

made any sense. The international organization wanted vengeance, and it wanted to send a message—mess with us and you disappear. Disappear to what? She could guess what their plan was for her.

Footsteps sounded outside the door.

Jennifer needed every advantage she could get. She closed her eyes, breathed slowly, and kept her face towards the door.

The door opened.

Cracking her eyelids was a risk. She took it.

A man stood studying her. He was tall. No, long. He was long and skinny. Though he stood upright, something about the man reminded her of a snake.

No doubt a poisonous one.

She memorized his description and named him Viper.

Viper turned to someone behind him, someone outside the door. "She's still out. That was a strong dose for a small woman. But she's breathing OK. Let's give her another hour, then we'll try waking her."

His voice sounded like a snake, more air than vocal chords. She heard the other voice. "Close the door, Snake."

Despite her situation, she bit her tongue to stifle a laugh.

Idiot, you don't need to chew on your tongue. Your mouth is taped. But Snake? No. I'll stick with Viper.

The conversation continued. The second man had an accent. Maybe Chinese. She would call him Mao and pray he wasn't as ruthless as his namesake.

She needed to focus, to glean any intelligence she could, any details of her whereabouts, and of their plans.

Mao continued talking. "We can't move her now.

The boss said to wait. Some do-gooder saw us take her and thought she was a teenager. Now we have an Amber Alert to deal with. The Feds locked down the whole island."

"We'll have to keep her at the house until we can move her to the yacht. But we can't wait forever. The FBI is more likely to show up here than on the yacht," Viper said in a voice that was breathy, almost a hiss.

The man's voice drove a shiver down her spine. She needed to escape before Viper could strike.

The conversation had ended. The footsteps moved away from the door.

So she was in a house. Jennifer looked around.

She was in a bedroom, a dark bedroom. They worried about the house being found. It must be in Kihei, near where they took her.

The move to a yacht worried her. Once they moved her, she could be in international waters, and beyond help, in less than two hours. Would an Amber Alert prevent that?

Lee. Tears filled her eyes. He would be worried sick, and he would never give up trying to find her. He could be in danger, too. She needed help and sought it from the only One Who could help her when she was so helpless.

Please be with Lee. He needs Your help now more than ever. Keep him safe and me, too. Thanks for the Amber Alert. It buys us some time.

Jennifer inventoried her advantages. She was intelligent, but her captors probably knew about that. There would be no chess games unless the game started with her in checkmate. However, they probably didn't know she could defend herself. The only two traffickers who knew about that, the two she had kicked, were dead.

What should she do now? She needed to appear physically weak, to cower at physical threats, and to wait for an opportunity to escape. Hopefully she would find a situation where she only needed to take out one person.

To prepare for an opportune moment, she iterated through a list of the most vicious defensive maneuvers Granddad had taught her.

Whether Jennifer was on land or water, the biggest obstacle to escaping alive was the band around her wrists. Solving the wrist-band problem was her first priority—correction, it was her second priority. She looked upward and focused on her first priority.

When it's the right time, please, Lord, show me the way to escape.

6

Nearly three hours had passed since Jennifer was taken. Lee had learned that in the interim the Maui Police Department, including their Investigative Services Bureau, as well as the FBI and the Coast Guard, were involved in the search for Jennifer. So far, there were no breaks in the case, at least nothing he was told about.

Detective Ramirez had dispatched Officers Yagi and Kaai to take Lee back to Kihei. The normally talkative Yagi was silent as the patrol car rolled along the highway between Wailuku and Kihei. The questions had all been asked, and there was no news to discuss.

Lee was also silent as he tried to come up with his own plan to end this nightmare.

A few minutes down the road, Yagi broke the silence. "It's been a tough evening for us all, and it'll probably be a long night for every cop on the island. Brandt, you need to go back to your room and try to get some rest. Like Ramirez said, if something breaks, we'll let you know."

"Yeah. It's going to be a long night." But there was no way he could rest, and going back to the room would only drive him crazy with thoughts and worries about Jennifer. He could feel her in his arms like she was minutes before she vanished. He'd already been driven crazy, he just hadn't admitted to himself. "Will you guys please drop me off at the lot north of the shops? That's where I parked our car."

As they approached the north end of town, Kaai veered left onto Highway 31 to bypass the downtown area. A few lights later, he turned right, and they descended the hill, heading into town.

As they approached South Kihei Road, Lee recognized their location. "Our car is in the lot on the right, about half a block ahead."

After Kaai stopped the patrol car in the parking lot, and Yagi opened the door, Lee hopped out of the confining back seat. "Thanks guys. Let me know the minute you hear anything, OK?"

"Sure thing," Yagi said. "Now you try to get some rest. Let us and the Feds do what we do best, catch the bad guys."

If they were trying to encourage him, it wasn't working. "Yeah. I'll try."

Lee unlocked the door of the rental car and slid in. The tropical fruit fragrance of Jennifer's lotion lingered in the car. It created an ache so intense and deep inside that breathing took effort.

Panic, depression, and nausea assaulted him in a physically and emotionally crippling sequence. Lee swallowed hard and fought off the urge to vomit. His feelings of helplessness and hopelessness were overwhelming. He had to do something now, or it would send him to a place he couldn't afford to go. Sleep, that was out of the question. So was going back to the room where he and Jennifer had planned to spend their wedding night. Wedding night…nightmare. If only he could wake up and end the dream. That wasn't going to happen unless he *made* it happen.

He started the car, turned right out of the lot, and then went left on South Kihei Road, looking for a place to think, to get some coffee, and to plan.

Less than a mile down the road, he came to a strip mall on the left hosting a twenty-four hour restaurant. In an hour or so, there would be nothing else open. The restaurant seemed made to order. He turned in and parked.

Lee walked into the place and looked for a suitable table, one like him, alone and in a corner.

With only a half dozen other customers in the place, a waitress soon spotted him at his table. "Aloha and good evening. What can I get for—"

"Coffee. Black, please. That's all." He didn't feel the spirit of aloha tonight and it wasn't a good evening.

The change in the waitress's expression told him she got the message. "Coffee, coming right up."

After the waitress wheeled and strode away, his spot in the corner seemed too confining. It was closing in on him. He felt uneasy, claustrophobic. He had to move. Now.

When Lee stood, he was panting, struggling to breathe. He needed to settle down and think, or he would be no good to Jennifer. No good to anybody. He sat back down.

A thought, perhaps a voice, sounded in his troubled mind, reverberating inside his heart. *Do you trust Me?*

"Yes," he whispered without hesitation, without thinking.

Even in light of this?

He couldn't answer. His own heart convicted him. Yes, he trusted God within limits, within the comfort zone of Lee Brandt's normal, tidy life. But this was a violation of trust, a violation of love, a violation of goodness.

But who is violating goodness?

Lee shoved the intruding thought from his mind when he shoved his chair back from the table and left the corner and the thoughts that were suffocating him.

He moved to a table in the middle of the room.

Two tables away, a young girl about Katie's age, maybe sixteen, sat with a man twice her age. The muscular man in dark cargo shorts and a black T-shirt looked out of place with the young girl.

Even here inside the restaurant he couldn't escape the reminders of Jennifer's abduction. The man fit the meager description Yagi had provided, but...no, he was obsessed with finding Jennifer's captors, and he was just being stupid. This was not the perp, and he couldn't waste time with useless—

He jumped when a coffee cup thumped on the table. He tried to give the waitress a smile, but he had no clue what expression his face held.

"You're welcome," the waitress replied, then scurried away as if to be rid of him.

"Can't move her now..." A man's voice.

Lee turned his head to see where the softly spoken words had come from. The man sitting beside the teenage girl. It must have been him. Lee stared at his coffee cup and strained to hear more.

"...stay in the house until..."

"...island's sealed..."

Both times it was the man's voice. Were the phrases he overheard coincidence or, as unlikely as it seemed, were the two speaking about Jennifer? He had to know. Lee quickly appended two more actions onto his slowly developing plan.

He initiated the first action by slipping his cell phone from his pocket. Moving his thumbs, he tried to imitate someone texting. Instead of pressing letters, he put his cell in camera mode and moved it until the man and the girl were centered on the display. He pressed the button to capture the image.

When the picture appeared, it looked clear. He could see the sides of both faces and a profile of their bodies. He saved the picture, then looked up at the couple's table, positioning his cell to take another. They were gone.

Lee quickly scanned the room.

The two were approaching the exit door.

He pulled a five spot from his wallet, tossed it on the table, and hurried after them.

After he stepped outside, Lee had to pause while his eyes adjusted to the dimly lit parking lot. He scanned the entire area. The two people were nowhere in sight.

Only one route could have allowed them to disappear so quickly. They had gone around the corner, behind the building.

He ran to the corner of the restaurant and looked into the darkness behind it. Without scaling a six-foot fence, there was only one path they could have taken. They had crossed an undeveloped field that sloped upward towards a residential area.

A residential area? The words "Can't move her now…stay in the house…" replayed in his mind as he stared into the darkness.

7

Lee stared across the dark, undeveloped field populated with scrubby bushes large enough to hide two people. Beyond the big field there were condos on the left side, houses at the far end, and a tall fence on the right side.

The house that the man and the girl came from was probably a short walk away. But based only on the few words he had heard, Lee couldn't be certain these people were the perps. There was, however, something he could do about his uncertainty.

I can remove it.

He pulled out his cell phone and the piece of computer paper he had stuffed into his pocket. He studied the picture on his cell and read the words written on the paper, Grand Wailea Resort.

Lee looked at his watch. Ten forty-five PM. Unless she was a night owl, Bertha Renner would soon get a wake-up call.

Lee wheeled and trotted to his car. When he pulled out of the restaurant parking lot, he headed south towards Wailea, disregarding the twenty-five-mile-per-hour speed limit signs.

Within five minutes, his headlights illuminated a sign pointing to the Grand Wailea Resort. Even without the sign Lee would've recognized the large resort by the myriad lights coming from the tall, wide building. He parked in the first parking spot he found, a spot reserved for hotel guests. He wasn't concerned about his car being towed because he wouldn't be here that long.

Shortly after entering the main entrance, Lee spotted a resort directory on the wall near an elevator. He located the Chapel Wing and took the elevator to the fourth floor.

When he exited the elevator, a sign directed him towards Bertha Renner's room number. He counted the room numbers up to 414 and stopped. His watch said 10:55 PM when he knocked on her door.

No response. Had he interpreted Ramirez's note correctly?

He knocked again, louder this time.

Someone was stirring inside. Soon the door moved slightly outward. Someone had pushed against it.

He pulled his engagement picture from his wallet and held it about eighteen inches from the peephole.

An unintelligible exclamation came from inside. The deadbolt clicked and the door swung open.

In the doorway, wrapped in a robe, stood a middle-aged lady wearing a sympathetic expression.

That puzzled him.

"You must be her husband," the woman said.

Husband? How did she know? The Amber Alert was still in effect. No one should know Jennifer was married.

She was frowning.

He needed to say something. "And your name must be Bertha Renner. But how did you know she had a husband?"

"I've been watching the news to see if the police caught those people and freed the girl."

This was not good. Too much had been leaked to

the media. On the other hand, if the goons thought the alert was over and some of the pressure was off, they might try to move Jennifer. If they did, they might get caught in the process because the pressure wasn't off. It would only intensify, and when Peterson arrived, the pressure would become incredible.

"Young man, I'm talking to you. What's your name?" The woman's frown remained.

"Sorry, ma'am. I'm Lee Brandt, and the woman you saw taken is my wife. We were married earlier today, and we're here on our honeymoon."

"I am *so* sorry. I've been praying for the girl. Now I'll pray for you both." She pursed her lips, but the frown was replaced by a warm sympathetic expression.

"Thanks a lot, ma'am. But there is something else you can do that might really help this investigation."

Her eyes widened. "What's that? I'll be glad to help if I can."

He pulled out his cell and brought up the picture of the two people in the restaurant. He stepped beside her, turned it towards Mrs. Renner, and pointed to the darkly clad man. "Do you recognize him?"

"Oh my. Oh *my*," She exclaimed in wide-eyed horror. "I recognize them both,"

Both? "Do you mean the girl was involved in the abduction?"

Mrs. Renner nodded. "She stayed in the background while the man in the picture hooked your wife's throat with his arm. He choked her and, in a few seconds, she fell. A second man helped catch her, and then the two men carried her into the dark parking lot. The girl stayed in the background, like she was watching. She looked right at me once and I thought I was going to have a heart attack."

The choking hold had to be the LVNR, lateral vascular neck restraint, the sleeper hold. Was that what Yagi had neglected to tell him? It was how they took Katie in Seattle. If Yagi had told Lee, it would have provided the first link to the Seattle-area traffickers, their MO. But he shouldn't fault Yagi. The man was just doing his job and trying to be kind by sparing Lee the ugly details.

"Thanks, ma'am. You've really helped this investigation. When we free Jennifer, you'll get personal thanks from both of us." He tried to give her a smile, but even this break didn't alleviate the panic in his heart. But it did send it racing.

"You're welcome, Mr. Brandt. I'll be right here if you wish to find me...for the next three wonderful weeks. And I'll be praying they turn out wonderful for you and your wife."

"Thanks again." Lee hurried down the hall and keyed in the number on the card that Detective Ramirez had given him.

This could be the first big break in the case, but how would the police react to it coming from Lee's personal investigation? They would probably get mad and reprimand him. But would they believe him? Listen to him? If so, how quickly would they respond?

8

For what seemed like hours, Jennifer lay on the floor trying to loosen or break the restraining band around her wrists. She had only succeeded in rubbing her wrists raw. The stinging grew intense and the restraints grew sticky against her wrists. Her wrists…they were bleeding. She'd long since given up on the double restraints around her ankles.

She could see the room in more detail than an hour ago. The edges of the heavy curtains were lined with light. Not direct sunlight, perhaps the light of dawn. But her search of the dark room revealed nothing she could use to cut or abrade the restraints.

Jennifer's stomach growled, and her tongue stuck to the roof of her mouth. Food and water. She would have to steel herself against the deprivation of both. Her captors were anything but compassionate people.

Footsteps sounded outside the room. Jennifer shot a prayer for strength heavenward, and prepared for something unpleasant…or worse.

Two strong-looking men entered. The one in front brandished a large knife, and he carried it like he meant to use it. Probably for intimidation. That's how she preferred to interpret his posture and his grip on the knife.

The overhead lights came on. She squinted to shield her eyes against the brightness. Then she smelled the food. The second man carried a plate with some kind of a meal and a glass of water. So they meant to keep her alive. That meant they would probably—she shoved the disquieting thought from her mind.

"Looks like our million-dollar baby is awake," the man with the big knife remarked while his eyes studied her body.

Mack...Mack the knife. That's what she would call him.

The second man set the plate on a dresser. "Let's see if she likes my cooking, Mack."

Mack...with a knife. She almost laughed. *I'm getting good at this.* Guessing her captors names—it was something she had no desire to do, let alone excel at.

The cook. She named him *Cook* and hoped he deserved his name.

"Just a minute," Mack said. "I need to tell her the rules." He sneered at her. "And the penalty for breaking them."

Jennifer lay on her side on the floor and prepared for intimidation of the worst sort.

Mack bent down and pushed the point of the knife to her throat near her jugular vein. "I'm going to remove the tape from your mouth." He paused, then swiveled and knelt behind her.

The knife also moved. Its point pricked the skin on her lower back. She felt pressure, then a burning pain.

Mack spoke. "That was only a sample. If you speak or make any sound above a whisper, this knife will sever your spinal cord. And you'll be...frankly, a worthless piece of sub-human flesh." His voice rose in volume and intensity. "Do you understand?"

Jennifer nodded. This guy was good at intimidation. He was also making her angry. She stifled the anger before it could bring her more trouble.

"Good," Mack said. "Now this will probably hurt. Cowboy up, baby, and be quiet."

Cowboy up? She filed the regional phrase away for future reference.

Mack ripped the tape from her mouth.

The sting felt like he'd ripped the skin from her face. She gasped and clamped her mouth shut to protect her stinging lips. Jennifer lay on the floor, clenching her jaw and breathing hard through her nose. As the pain subsided, she opened her mouth to breathe more fully.

"Look at those lips. The rest of her face, too," Cook said.

"Cool it, Cookie. You can't have her. Now, million-dollar baby, you look old enough to feed yourself, so I'm going to cut your hands loose...on two conditions. Rather, one condition with two penalties. The condition, you use your hands only to feed yourself. The knife stays on your spine. One wrong move and I push it." He paused. "Oh, yes. The other penalty. We'll take your blonde-haired princess and sell her to the people who originally ordered her. They're still waiting for delivery."

Jennifer's head involuntarily jerked around, and she glared at Mack, biting her tongue to keep from painting him slime green with a dozen or more choice words that popped into her mind. How did they know about Katie? They wouldn't have unless they were the customers with the shopping list that, six weeks ago had Katie on it. A shopping list for people. Girls. Age, height, hair and eye colors, weight... Jennifer had to quit before she vomited.

"I see a rebellious spirit in this one, Cookie." He

put pressure on the knife.

Jennifer winced at the pain. She tried to stop the tears but her eyes brimmed with them. She managed to keep her mouth clamped shut. Right now, her mouth could get her in a lot of trouble, and she had just the words to incite it.

"Do you understand the penalties?"

Jennifer took a breath and nodded.

"Let me hear it, baby."

Though it galled her, she would comply "Yes, I understand," she whispered. "But how did you know about—"

"Shut up!"

She winced again from the stinging on her back when the knife pressed hard. So hard she expected it to enter her body at any moment.

"Let's just say we do our homework…thoroughly. Now eat, drink, and be mute."

Mack thinks he's clever. Maybe he would get a little too clever and slip up.

Mack sliced through the bands around her wrists, pulled her to her feet, and sat her in a chair. The knife returned to its place against her spine.

Jennifer looked at her wrists. They were raw and bleeding. She massaged them gingerly, avoiding the open abrasions.

"You keep trying that with your hands and you'll cut'em off," Cook said, laughing softly.

"You'd better listen to Cookie," Mack said. "Or I'll cut them off for you. Now eat."

She had felt twinges of hunger until the last exchange with Mack. Now the bacon, eggs, and toast made her swallow hard to keep from vomiting.

But Mack had given the order to eat and he'd

threatened Katie. Jennifer couldn't let anything happen to the precious, beautiful young lady soon to be her daughter. And Lee's. The two men might be bluffing about Katie, but she wouldn't take that chance.

Jennifer took the fork, then a bite of egg, all the time fighting the urge to throw it back up. After a couple of bites of toast, the nausea eased. She took a few more bites of egg and downed a piece of bacon.

Suddenly, she was ravenous. So hungry she felt guilty that the threat to Katie no longer made her sick. That was idiotic. She needed her strength.

She drank the water while Cook leered at her. She couldn't read his disgusting thoughts, but realizing he had them, her nausea returned. Jennifer locked gazes with Cook and glared at him, trying to look brave. But she prayed she would not be left alone in a room with him. Not unless her hands and feet were free.

Mack stepped in front of the chair, snatched the plate, and handed it to Cook. The knife was at her throat now.

"That's enough. Can't have our million-dollar baby losing her million-dollar figure, can we?" He sneered at her. "Hands behind your back and keep quiet."

Slowly she complied, dreading the raw burning the plastic restraints would soon produce. The knife moved away from her throat.

She gasped, as pain shot through her trembling hands when Mack pulled the restraints even tighter than before. The man thrived on cruelty.

"No more games, baby." The knife stung as it pricked her back again. "Since you like those lips, Cookie, maybe you should be the one to cover them up with the tape, you know, to remove the temptation."

"Emotionally incontinent goon." Had she uttered those words or just thought them?

"What did you just mutter, baby?" Mack asked, the edge on his voice as sharp as the knife pressing into her back.

She paused, searching for words that wouldn't be inflammatory.

"I asked you a question." Mack pushed harder on the knife.

"I...I called Cookie...emotionally incontinent." She pursed her lips and waited for something extremely unpleasant.

A loud, mirthless laughing noise came from Mack's mouth. "She has quite a vocabulary, Cookie." He laughed again, like the staccato barking of a dog. "And she's got your number. But *sexually* incontinent would be more accurate."

Cookie traced her lips with his finger, then slapped a piece of duct tape over her mouth, smoothing it out on her cheeks.

"You can play doctor now, if you'd like, Cookie." Mack's voice became soft and pleasant. He was mocking Cook.

Cook reached for a small container on the dresser. He opened it and pulled out a syringe. After filling it, he moved towards her.

Not this again. Drugs were something she could not fight.

"Wait a minute. We can't have her falling and getting hurt. Not this million-dollar baby."

Mack put down his knife, picked her up, and laid her on the floor. "Roll onto your stomach."

When she complied, Jennifer felt helpless, hopeless. Tears filled her eyes. More drugs were coming. She had missed her opportunity to escape.

Cook plunged the needle deep into the back of her shoulder. The sting intensified as his pressure blasted the solution into her muscle tissue.

In a few seconds, her thoughts became slow, difficult, at the mercy of the drugs.

I'm so sorry, Lee. I tried to escape. I tried so hard...

9

A measure of hope returned as Lee realized the potential of the information he had stumbled upon. A quick response by the police could bring the result he prayed for, Jennifer's safe return.

Standing outside of the Grand Wailea Resort, he keyed in Detective Ramirez's number, pressed the send icon, and waited.

Ramirez answered on the second ring.

"Ramirez, this is Lee Brandt. I've found the goons who took Jennifer."

Silence.

"Look, Brandt, we have a multi-organizational operation going here. I don't have time for amateur det—"

"Ramirez!" The name exploded from Lee's pent-up emotions. "Maybe I should be calling you the amateur. I have a positive ID on two of the perps, and I know approximately where they are."

"What do you mean by positive ID?" Ramirez's voice still sounded condescending, like he was talking to a child.

That pushed Lee over the edge. "Look, you knucklehead! I have a picture of one of the men and the girl who abducted—"

"How did you know about the girl?" The speaker on his phone popped as each word exploded from Ramirez's mouth. "We didn't release that

49

information."

"Bertha Renner told me when I showed her a picture of the man and the girl, the picture I took with my cell."

"Brandt, you were supposed to be waiting in your room while we—"

"While you what? Solved the case? Maybe now you can. Do you want the picture and the info, or not? If you aren't going to act on it, I am." He was on the verge of saying things he would more than just regret, things with immediate consequences.

"I can have you locked up, Brandt. Don't try playing maverick cop on me."

"I'm not a cop, Ramirez. But I've probably seen more action on big cases over the last nine months than any of your men. If you're going to try to stop me, you'll have to catch me first. Is that really how you want to use your resources right now? Besides, I can go to the press with—"

"OK! OK! Tell me what you have." Ramirez's voice softened. "I'll listen."

Lee took a calming breath, then related what he had overheard at the restaurant. He recounted in detail Bertha Renner's response to seeing the picture. And he told Ramirez about the residential area the man and the girl headed towards when they disappeared.

When Lee finished, he waited for a response.

Silence again.

Ramirez cleared his throat. "Sounds like we got our first beak in this case."

"No kidding." Lee wanted the words back the moment he uttered them. "Sorry, Ramirez. When the person you love more than life is stolen on your wedding night, it can make a person a little—"

"A little crazy?"

"Yeah. A lot crazy. Look…I couldn't sleep and found an all-night restaurant. I was drinking coffee and just stumbled onto this. Some people might call it luck, but there are people praying for Jennifer. I don't know how you see it, but I don't believe my overhearing this conversation was mere coincidence. Now, do you want the picture of the two suspects?"

"Yes. Of course I want it."

"I can e-mail it to you right now if—"

"Send it. Ramirez at Maui PD dot com. I'll make sure it gets a speedy distribution. By the way, a tall FBI agent got here a while ago."

"Peterson?"

"Yeah. As soon as we're all on the same page here, he said he'd call you. Thought you would want to know."

"He has my cell number. We've worked together on a couple of cases. Is Peterson with you now?"

"He's somewhere in the building. I'll fill him in when I see him."

"OK. I'm going to hang up now, so I can send you the picture."

****

Ten minutes later, Lee drove northbound on South Kihei Road, debating what he should do next, when his cell rang. He pulled onto the shoulder and opened his cell.

"Lee, this is Peterson."

"According to Ramirez you've been here a while getting up to speed. Speaking of speed, you must have had a lot of that on your way here."

Peterson gave a half-hearted chuckle. "Like I said earlier, they're pulling out all of the stops to get Jennifer back."

Everything pointed to the fact that Peterson was withholding information, information that could help solidify Lee's plan. "Peterson, Joe Morrison at National Aerospace told me about how badly you wanted to rescue Jennifer last March. How her rescue had priority over mine. With the terrorists after us, she was a major national security concern. This isn't about—"

"Lee, don't ask, because I can't tell you much. Now, I'm going to—"

"This is more than a mission to stop an international human trafficking syndicate, isn't it?"

No reply.

"Peterson, I'm cleared above Top Secret, and I have a need to know. She's my wife. If there's something else going on here, tell me what you can. Please."

Peterson cleared his throat. "Lee, this isn't exactly a secure communication channel. But I can tell you this. A foreign government has agents on the island. We think they might make an offer for Jennifer...a much bigger offer than the trafficker's clients."

Lee was too stunned to reply. The nightmare grew more frightening with each bit of information he learned.

Peterson continued. "How they knew about Jennifer's capture, we don't know. But as they say, birds of a feather—"

"Not birds. You mean slime of the same shade of green."

"Something like that." Peterson sighed.

Jennifer's recent work on cellular- and wireless-intercept analysis was primarily aimed at tracking terrorists. A picture was coming into focus, a dark, ugly picture. Lee's gut told him the general answer, and the news media had recently provided some of the specifics. He had to ask the question, even if Peterson wouldn't or couldn't answer it.

"The foreign government you mentioned...it's Iran isn't it?"

Silence.

"You don't need to answer. Just find her, Peterson. Please. Just find her...soon."

What these people would want from Jennifer and what they would take from her to get it—he couldn't let his mind go there.

10

What were they doing to her? The question shot like a lightning bolt from the clouded thoughts in Jennifer's mind. The cloudy mind and the feelings were familiar. She had been drugged.

Clarity returned more quickly this time. Was that a good thing? Probably not. Her body was developing a tolerance to the drug. She prayed it wouldn't become a dependence.

Hands under her arms lifted her upper body. "Hurry," a hissing voice said, "It's going to be light soon. We've got to get her on the boat now."

Her eyes popped open. She stared into the face of a man who was lifting her legs and gawking at her. Cook. A quick foot stomp would do some serious damage to his face. She was tempted, but she wasn't a fool. She needed them to view her as helpless and harmless.

Jennifer raised her head. She looked out the open rear door of a van at a large, wooden crate lying on the ground. The crate appeared to be about six feet by—

"No!" she tried to yell, but her voice was muffled by the tape over her mouth. Panic at seeing the box ignited the fuse. Realization that they were carrying her to it, triggered the explosion in her mind.

For some reason her hands were free. She gestured frantically pointing to the box while whipping her head from side to side.

"So you don't want to take a trip in the box?" Snake hissed. He dropped her upper body onto the floor of the van and pulled out a knife.

She stopped struggling with the man, but tried to pull the tape from her mouth.

"And now you want the tape off." He grabbed her wrist and pulled her hand from her mouth. "You weren't supposed to be awake yet, Miss Universe."

She reached for the tape with her other hand. The knife pressed against her neck. She stopped moving.

"There's a quick, easy way to do this without using the box. But first, you've got to promise me you'll be absolutely silent if I remove the tape."

He pricked the skin on her throat with his knife. "You will remain quiet. Are we agreed?"

When he pulled the knife away from her throat, she nodded.

This guy must have taken lessons from Mack. Or perhaps they were both taught by the same master, the father of lies, the original snake.

Snake placed the cold blade against her neck. "Pull off the tape, Cookie. But Miss U needs to keep her head still or she might cut her own throat."

Cook pulled the tape from her mouth in one long, steady motion that seemed to peel the skin from her lips.

She closed her eyes, unable to stop the tears.

When she opened them, Snake stared into her eyes. It was a cold, deadly stare, like a viper ready to strike. "No talking except to answer my questions. Is that understood?"

"Yes." She spoke softly through raw, stinging lips.

Snake pulled her into a sitting position on the back of the van.

Jennifer took in as much of her surroundings as she could despite Snake's body shielding it from view. In the early morning light, she could distinguish the dark silhouette of a building off to the left. It resembled the old Congregational Church in Makena. To the right was water. They must be in Makena.

"Here's the plan, Miss U." Snake's reptilian voice and his lifeless stare made her shiver. "I stand you up, and then I'll slip behind you. The knife will be against your spinal cord, you know, that bundle of nerves I'm sure you want to keep intact. We'll walk together down to the water and up the ramp into the boat. Walk normally or you might never walk again."

The boat landing in Makena—she was certain of their location. But where were they taking her? Was there still an Amber Alert? Was the island locked down? It must be. They were using the semi-darkness to move her.

"Are you ready?"

He used no S-words, but still his voice sounded like a hiss. She needed to forget about his voice, to focus. Her hands were free for the moment, maybe she could use them to—

"I asked you a question."

Jennifer felt the breath of the hissing voice on her cheek. She pulled her head away from him. "Yes. I'm ready."

When Snake pulled her to her feet and slipped behind her, Jennifer peered through the dim light of early dawn at a Catamaran near the shore. How deep was the water where the ramp connected to the boat? Deep enough to dive in?

She felt a tug on her belt. Snake's hand had gripped it. A stinging chill ran up her spine as he pushed the knifepoint into her skin.

"Walk," he ordered.

Cook led the way, a few feet ahead of her. Snake walked close behind with a firm grip on her belt. She had perhaps thirty seconds to decide what to do, or it would be decided for her.

Jennifer quickly considered her options as they walked towards the water's edge. If she tried to escape, they would probably hesitate before deciding to kill her. She was worth a lot of money to them alive, nothing if she was dead. If she surprised them, their hesitation might give her time to escape.

She now had twenty seconds at most. To dive into the water she would have to break Snake's grip on her belt. Could she deliver a foot stomp without forcing the knife into her back in the process? Could she swim underwater far enough to escape? Too many variables in the equation.

Only ten seconds now.

A voice came from the Catamaran. "Hurry up. The tide's going out. We've got less than four feet of water under us."

She had only five seconds. But it no longer mattered, unless she wanted to break her neck by diving into the shallow water.

Did she want to break her neck? The thought crossed Jennifer's mind and lodged there as she walked up the ramp to the boat. Knowing the life she would be sold into, could she kill herself if there was no way of escape? It would be wrong. Life and death choices belonged to God. But would God forgive her if she did? She pushed these thoughts from her mind and tried to cling to the hope of rescue or escape.

She thought of Lee, of being his. One thing was

non-negotiable. Whatever it took, she would never belong to anyone but him. She would fight them savagely until she prevailed or they decided to kill her. *Please, God. Don't let it come to that.*

As Jennifer stepped onto the boat, out of sight of anyone on the shore, the restraints were again cinched tightly around her wrists and ankles. The tape was returned to her mouth.

The boat moved seaward, and Snake sat beside her prodding her with his knife. He looked up towards the boat's captain. "We've got only fifteen minutes before it's too light. You need to hurry."

"I cannot draw too much attention to us." The words came from a short, bald Asian man who was at the wheel of the boat. "We will be hidden by the yacht when we unload our…cargo. Do not worry."

In a few minutes, she glanced out the window. Above her she saw the shadowy outline of a much larger vessel against the steadily brightening sky. The yacht. This must be their client's vessel, the place where they would sell her, and she would begin her life of slavery. Once again she had missed her chance to escape. Possibly her last chance.

11

Lee gazed out the window of the restaurant into the darkness outside. It seemed that he was looking into the part of his heart where hope resided. Six AM. It was still too dark to see beyond the lighted parking lot. He was all out of ideas for his investigation. To burn up his nervous energy, he was spinning his cell in his hand, contemplating calling Ramirez for an update on the investigation.

The phone rang, startling him. He nearly dropped it onto the floor. It had been silent since 3:00 AM when Ramirez called to tell him the police were following several leads but still hadn't found the men who took Jennifer.

Lee glanced at the caller ID. A local number. His heart sank. He answered but with a lackluster greeting.

"Lee, this is Granddad. Katie and I are at the airport renting a car."

"I didn't expect you this soon."

"We caught a flight that was delayed from earlier in the evening. It saved us two hours. Do you have any more news about Jennifer?"

He looked around the restaurant at the thirty or more customers. His gut told him to keep his voice down and choose his words carefully. "I stumbled onto some information that may give us a break in the case. We haven't found Jennifer yet, but let's rendezvous here in Kihei, and I'll fill you in. I think we need to do some investigating of our own."

"Katie and I would like that. We need to do something to help after sitting helpless on a plane for six hours. We're both sick with worry."

"Do you know where Starbucks on South Kihei Road is located?"

"I know that area. My cousin runs a boat rental at the marina in Kihei a few blocks from there."

"Meet me there as soon as you can."

"OK. But first someone here needs to talk to you."

"Lee, it's Katie. I prayed for Jenn all the way here. I made a real nuisance of myself with God."

"Me too, Katie. I pestered Him all night. I love you, girl. See you in a few minutes, and we'll talk about what we need to do next." Hearing her voice and realizing she was now on Maui drove another spike of fear into his stomach. Come what may, he must protect Katie.

Lee closed his cell, left a generous tip for the waitress who had kept his coffee cup filled much of the night, and headed for his rental car.

In the predawn light, he drove north to the coffee shop while he sorted through the fragments of information he would soon share with Granddad and Katie. From the information, Lee tried to develop a plan of action. But when he turned in at the Kukui Mall and parked, his plan was mostly a wish list. To turn his wishes into something solid—

What I need is a lamp, one with a genie. Or the real thing, an angel from God.

12

After Snake pulled her onto her feet, Jennifer surveyed the view from the nearest window in the catamaran, trying to determine what lay ahead, but fear threatened to paralyze her mind and suck the strength from her body.

"Keep moving, keep quiet, and don't try anything stupid." Snake prodded her from behind. "Rumor has it you're a million-dollar baby. Personally, I don't think you're worth it."

Jennifer turned her head and glared at him. She couldn't care less what he thought.

"I see you disagree with my assessment." He gave her a thin-lipped smile.

Too many Ss. Snake's incessant hissing was grating on her nerves.

"Beauty is in the eye of beholder, so all that matters is what our client thinks you're worth." He pushed her towards the cabin door.

Jennifer glanced out another window. High above, the sky was already a bright blue. Another beautiful day in paradise. It was the antithesis for her, bound with nylon restraints.

She scanned the dark outline of Haleakala through the window. The volcanic mountain filled half of the sky, blocking the sun, protracting the dawn, betraying her by giving her captors enough time to move her.

Molikini lay to the southwest, so the yacht must be

anchored off the northern part of Makena or the southern part of Wailea. If she swam, the nearest point to land would be either somewhere near the Grand Wailea Resort or more to the south, where a point jutted out into the water near the Makena Beach Resort. But knowing her location did her no good unless she could free her hands.

She studied Snake again as he pulled her towards a ramp, temporarily connecting the catamaran to the yacht. Vicious at first, the man had become cocky. If her hands were free, her kick would smash his face and the evil smirk it wore, knocking the vile man into the water. Then she would dive in on the opposite side of the ramp.

She visualized her stance and the ferocious kick. Then saw herself drown without hands free to swim. Somehow the restraining bands had to come off.

Snake pushed her up the ramp with his knife. "Whatever you're thinking, I wouldn't try it. Move. Faster."

Clearly they wanted to transfer her quickly, while the yacht blocked the view of anyone on the shore and before the sun popped over the mountain.

Jennifer slowed, testing them, trying to make something happen, and immediately felt pressure from the knife against her spine. Feeling she had little to lose this point, she slowed further and gauged Snake's response.

The knife moved.

Pain radiated through her neck as the knife punctured her skin. Blood trickled down her neck, staining her tank top.

"Move."

"You fool!" The exclamation came from a booming

voice on the yacht. "Do not scar her. I do not deliver damaged goods." Those were Trader's words. *The company slogan?*

"Sorry, Mr. James. But she has become extremely uncooperative."

"Use your imagination, Snake. Not your knife. Do you understand?"

"Yes, sir." Snake leaned forward and hissed into her ear. "If I've scarred you too much, Cookie will still take you. He's got a hundred grand that he'd be delighted to spend...all for you."

She tried to ignore him while she moved slowly up the ramp towards the yacht. Snake was trying to play head games with her. She hoped he continued that approach. If he did, eventually he would lose. That and the fact that Mr. James had just robbed Snake of his preferred method of motivation, cruelty, gave her a small measure of hope.

At the end of the ramp, Jennifer stepped onto the yacht. The large, luxurious vessel had three or four rooms along the side where she had boarded. The owner, probably Mr. James, was obviously a man of wealth. Probably a man of power. He didn't appear to be the type who was enslaved to uncontrolled desires, like Cookie. But the desire for power and wealth could also enslave a person.

She glanced into Mr. James's eyes as she passed him. He had eyes the eyes of a hawk, seeing everything and seeing it as his prey. The man looked cold and calculating. No. James was not the consumer in this ugly economy.

Jennifer was certain she would be sold to someone else. That meant she still had some time. How much time? Would it be enough to escape? What if they drugged her again? If they did, she would be sold and could do nothing about it.

Drug me? I can't let that happen. Not at any cost.

14

Lee glanced up from his coffee cup when the door to the shop flew open. A tall, slender, blonde teenager wearing blue shorts and a white tank top zigzagged between chairs and tables and then threw her arms around him.

Tears fell onto his bare arms as Katie buried her face into the top of his shoulder. "Please tell me they found her, Lee, and that Jenn's OK."

Granddad's trim, fit seventy-two-year-old body quickly caught up with Katie. He met Lee's gaze with a face etched with lines of worry. "Is there any news?"

Lee stroked Katie's head and wiped her cheeks. "Yeah. There's some news, but let's get you two some caffeine, and then I'll catch you up on what's happening."

"I can't think about coffee until you tell us about the—"

Lee put his fingers over Katie's lips. "There are too many unfriendly eyes and ears on this island. The trouble is I can't tell our friends from our enemies. Let's get you some coffee and move to the tables outside. It's more…private."

Katie's eyes widened. "Do you mean that—"

"Yes. We need to talk privately. But first, let's order something to keep you two awake."

Katie rubbed her bare arms. It's wet here, like it's been raining. It's hot, too."

"It's called humidity, Katie. I'll order you something cold to drink. Black coffee for you, Granddad?"

"Yes, please." Granddad took Katie's arm and pulled her towards the door leading to the patio. "Katie and I will wait for you outside."

Lee turned to the barista.

The young man had clearly spotted Katie. His gaze followed her closely as he prepared their drinks.

Katie's beauty, grace, and elegance far exceeded her fifteen years. The man's scrutiny reminded Lee of the potential danger to her should they encounter the slimy form of humanity that sought to make merchandise of God's finest handiwork. He would keep her as far from danger as possible.

Juggling three drinks, Lee nudged the door open with his shoulder and stepped to the table where Katie and Granddad sat.

Katie rose to her feet. Her drawn face seemed to add years to her normally youthful appearance. The fear in her eyes ripped at Lee's heart. Like Jennifer, Katie was fearless, except when those she loved were in danger and she couldn't help them. But maybe the "couldn't help them" part was about to change.

Lee handed them their coffee and all three huddled close around the small table. He met Katie's gaze. "Last night I saw two of the perps who took Jenn."

"You saw what?" Katie jumped to her feet. "Where did you—"

"Keep it down, Katie. We don't want to advertise what we're up to."

Katie sat down and their three heads leaned together in a tight circle.

Lee recounted events at the restaurant and ended with Bertha Renner's positive ID of two of the perpetrators.

"Did you say the girl was about sixteen and blonde?" Katie asked with a squinting frown.

"Yeah. Here, I'll show you." Lee pulled out his cell, zoomed in on the girl in the picture, and turned the display towards Katie.

"Anya!" The name blasted from Katie's mouth in a fierce whisper that sounded like it had come from a wild animal.

Lee ran her single-word outburst through his mind a second time before the full implication registered. There *was* a close tie to the traffickers in the Northwest.

He met Katie's gaze and smiled. "I think you're my genie."

"Jeannie? I hate that name. But that's Anya, and she helped them take me. And now Jenn."

"You're the genie who came out of a lamp and granted my wish. Actually you're my angel, the answer to my prayers."

She gave him a puzzled frown.

"Forget the metaphors, Katie." He draped an arm around her shoulders. "I need you to do something for me. Relax and concentrate on Anya. Tell me everything you know about her. You said she attended your school for three or four weeks. What did you learn about her?"

Katie let out a long sigh. "I didn't learn much. Now that I think about it, she didn't share much with me. But she did love coffee, mostly Starbucks' lattes. I wasn't into coffee then, but she sure was."

"Anything else, Katie? Anything at all?"

"No. That's it. She was friendly, but a little mysterious."

"So we have a girl who's staying in Kihei, who loves Starbucks coffee, and there are only two stores in town. Someone at one of the stores could recognize her. Maybe they can help us." Lee stood. "Come on. We're going inside."

His encounter with the two suspects at the restaurant was not coincidental. Maybe Katie's revelation while they sat outside the coffee shop wasn't either.

Granddad and Katie followed him to the patio door and into the shop. Business looked slow at the moment, so Lee walked up to the person tending the register, pulling Katie alongside. "Ma'am, we're looking for someone Katie here knows from the mainland. The young lady we're looking for loves her coffee." He turned the display on his cell towards the young woman at the register. "Do you recognize her?"

"Yes. She's been a regular here for at least a couple of weeks. In fact, Kevin"—she pointed towards the barista—"has asked her out on a date several times."

Lee glanced at Katie and saw excitement growing in her intense, blue eyes. "May we have a moment with Kevin?"

"I can trade positions with Kevin for a while. It'll be slow here for another hour." She turned towards the young man who was snapping a lid on a cup. "Hey, Kevin. Some people here would like to speak with you about a certain cute little blonde. You got a minute?"

Kevin slid the drink across the pick-up counter towards the only other customer in the shop. "Sure." He stepped towards them. "Are we talking about Anya?" His eyes darted between Lee and Katie.

"Yeah, Anya," Lee said.

"You know, she's older than she looks. She's nineteen," he said. "I asked her out, but no luck yet."

"Katie knows her from the mainland. But we don't have her address or phone number. Does she live up the hill from the twenty-four hour restaurant?" Lee pointed southward.

"Funny you should ask." Kevin frowned. "She gave me a phone number. I did a reverse lookup on the Internet and traced the phone number to a house. Yeah, it's up the hill from there." He paused. "I convinced her to let me walk her home from the shop once, and she went to a house in North Kihei. I never could figure out where she really lives." He shook his head. "She's a mysterious girl."

"Sometimes Anya is like that," Katie said. "You think you know her, then…" Katie shrugged.

"I guess we need to check out both places, if you want to visit with Anya, Katie." Lee looked up at the barista. "Can you show us where the two houses are?"

Kevin walked around the counter into the shop where a rack of tourist brochures stood against the wall. He pulled out one and unfolded it on a table, revealing a detailed map of Kihei. "Anybody got a pen?"

Lee pulled out his space pen and handed it to Kevin.

"I think the house I walked her to is right…here. It's tan colored and has a lot of vegetation around it…palm trees, bushes." He pulled out his wallet, slipped out a piece of paper, and copied an address onto the map. "Here's the other house in South Kihei."

Katie frowned at Kevin. "You aren't stalking her are you?"

"No. That's not my style. There just aren't many girls like her, even on Maui. However, with…uh, Katie, is it? There aren't any like you *anywhere* on the island."

Lee flinched at Kevin's overture. He leaned towards Kevin, but stopped when Katie shoved her palm at him.

She smiled and stared at the young man with cold steel in her blue eyes. "Yes, it's Katie. Anya might be older than she looks, but I'm a bit younger." She paused, her gaze locked on Kevin's. "By the way, the last man who threatened me, Lee split his head wide open and blood flew everywhere."

Kevin took a step back and his eyes widened.

"Granddad," she patted Granddad's shoulder, "has a sixth-degree black belt in karate. He can kick your head into orbit. I'm only fifteen, Kevin. But, when it's time for me to start courting, anyone who wants to see me has to go through both of them first." Katie's cold stare pushed the young barista further back until he banged into the counter, sending a cup of drink stoppers clattering across the shop floor.

"I only meant to, uh, pay you a compliment, Katie. I didn't mean—"

"And I only meant to spare you some serious grief. In four or five years, if you're still interested, you know who you need to talk to."

The first genuine smile in twelve hours spread across Lee's face.

The door popped open and two customers walked in.

"Thanks for your help, Kevin." Lee picked up the map of Kihei and took Katie's arm, leading the three back to the patio.

The hissing sound behind them wasn't steam from

the espresso machine, and it wasn't a truck's air brakes. It was Kevin's relief escaping, clearly audible above the din of the coffee shop.

On the patio, Lee stopped Katie, took her by the shoulders, and mouthed the words he said to her the first time she saved his life, "I'm so proud of you."

Katie's strong arms returned his hug with a fierceness few girls could match. Once again, tears fell on his bare arm.

When the three sat down at the table outside, Lee spread out the map and quickly located the approximate spot of the house in south Kihei. "I'll check the house at the south end of town and—"

"Then I'm going with you, Lee."

He studied Katie's face and the fiery look in her eyes. "You will go with Granddad."

"You're going there because that's where Anya went when she left the restaurant. That's where you think they're holding Jenn."

Lee turned his attention to Granddad. "Remember my conditions. I determine the line of fire."

Mr. Akihara placed a hand on Katie's shoulder. "Lee and I agreed on something, and I gave him my word, Katie. You wouldn't want to make me out to be a liar, would you?"

Her gaze dropped to the patio. Her shoulders drooped.

Lee sighed in relief. Katie was smart, passionate, and fearless. He believed she was also safe...for the time being.

It was only 7:30 AM. Too early to go knocking on doors.

Lee stepped inside the coffee shop and bought three breakfasts.

By the time they finished eating and planning, the warm sun had reached their table. It was 8:30.

"Time to go." Lee stood and drew Granddad's gaze. "Remember, Katie stays in the car and you go to the door."

"How can I forget? It's only the fifth time you've told me." Granddad smiled. "Don't worry, Lee. I will keep her safe."

When Lee turned left out of Kukui Center and headed towards the south end of town, he prayed he could keep Jennifer safe. Granddad looked like an Islander. He could walk up to the door without drawing much suspicion. But Lee's fading summer tan betrayed him. He was a mainlander, and he was known by the traffickers. He would be recognized. How could he approach the house without endangering Jennifer if she was inside?

15

On the deck of his yacht, Franklin James pored over the *Honolulu Star*, and the local daily paper, looking for news about the abducted girl, the girl now bound and gagged in a cabin on the yacht.

It was clever of the police to suppress information about her to keep the Amber Alert in effect and maintain the lockdown of the island. There had been only a few leaks to tip people that the alert was not warranted.

His cell phone lit up and played the theme from *The Munsters*. Nguyen. A repulsive song for a repulsive man.

"I was contacted by someone who wants to purchase your...merchandise. They appear knowledgeable about it. Too knowledgeable. We may have a problem." Nguyen sounded agitated, nervous.

First the Amber Alert and now this. James did not like surprises. "Meet me on my yacht as soon as possible and we will discuss this matter."

The unwelcome surprise took place on the island. He would ensure none took place aboard the yacht. James closed his cell and turned towards a crew member. "Snake."

"Yes, sir."

"As a precaution, watch any boats that approach us or that behave suspiciously. I want to know if anyone is watching us, even from a distance. Spread the word among the crew. Also, Nguyen is coming. Make sure he's alone. Don't let him on board if he's not."

"Sure thing, Mr. James." Snake replied in his peculiar, breathy voice.

Who were these people? He could find out. He was certain of that. But what worried him most was that they knew he had the girl.

James sat drumming out the rhythm of a galloping horse with his fingers on the deck table, trying to enumerate his options when Snake's voice interrupted his thoughts. "Mr. James," Snake hissed. "Nguyen is approaching and he's alone."

Nguyen pulled alongside the yacht. After Snake extended the ramp down to Nguyen's deck, the short, bowlegged man waddled up the ramp. When he stepped onto the deck, his bald brow wrinkled in a frown that reminded James of a shar-pei's head.

"Have a seat, Nguyen. Tell me everything you know about the people who contacted you, starting with their description."

"There were only two that I know of. One did all of the talking, and he had a dark complexion. Middle Eastern I think."

James sensed alarms sounding in his mind at the words Middle Eastern. Did they know about the prince? They could be his neighbors and competition among neighbors in the Middle East often went badly. James could be caught in the middle. He paused to clear his head. "How did they contact you?"

"I was eating breakfast at a restaurant in Wailea, and they just walked up to my table."

"Did they give you any clue how they knew to approach you or how they knew about our…merchandise?"

"I tried to coax that information from them, but they avoided my questions. They implied they knew a lot about us and sounded as if they were wealthy. They gave me a phone number to reach them."

"Calling them could be dangerous, could even be a trap." James paused to rethink the situation. "On the other hand, they already knew enough to trap us. They could have turned us in to the authorities. Since they haven't done that, I think perhaps they really do want to buy our merchandise, unless they are robbers who only want to steal it. Regardless, we know we have something they want…Jennifer Akihara-Brandt."

Nguyen sighed. "Should we do business with them? That is the first question."

"No, Nguyen. That is the second question. The first question is, how did they link us to the girl? If *they* can link us to the missing girl, so can others. I must talk to them. Middle Eastern…we may be dealing with some of the prince's neighbors, perhaps feuding neighbors. We must tread lightly."

Nguyen's bald pate wrinkled above widened eyes. "So you are going to call them?"

"No, Nguyen." He smiled. "*You* are going to call them…on your phone, and then hand the phone to me. Do it now, please."

Nguyen squirmed. Beads of perspiration appeared on his forehead. "Of course, Mr. James."

Any man who thought he was clever when he was not was a liability. One James could ill afford. Perhaps in a few months he would liquidate Nguyen's assets to pay for the liability.

Nguyen pulled a card from his pocket and reached for his cell.

"When you get them on the line," he paused, "let them know who you are, the man they met at the restaurant, then tell them you're passing them to your boss. Do you understand?"

Nguyen nodded and placed the call. Their customer answered promptly. After the introductions, Nguyen handed the phone to him.

"So, Mr. James, at last we talk."

He couldn't place the accent, but the fact that the man knew his name was of more concern. "You know who *I* am. It appears you have me at a disadvantage. Would you like to—"

"No, I wouldn't. I *like* having my partners at a disadvantage. But I will tell you this, I am someone who could be a very, very good customer. Someone willing to purchase certain merchandise which you have."

James sighed for effect. "I already have very good customers."

"But do you have anyone who will pay you four million dollars for Jennifer Akihara?"

Nguyen was right. They knew far too much, and they were a problem, a big problem. "So we finally get to the point. First, I should warn you." James paused. "She's not a teenage, exotic beauty, she's twenty-six and—"

"We understand. We want her for what she *knows*, not what she looks like, though her looks are, shall we say, extremely interesting."

"I'm afraid that's not the kind of business I'm in." *And not the kind I want to be in.*

"Maybe we want it to look like this is business as usual for you. Would five million help you make an exception to your business practices?"

"I only do business with people I trust. Only those who will bring me no trouble in return. You want her for what she knows. That could bring big trouble, the entire US government."

"In case you haven't noticed, Mr. James, part of the US government is already here. If you wait, more will come...NSA, the CIA, DHS to mention a few. Who knows, in a few hours Navy Seals could take your yacht before you even realize they're there. You don't have the luxury of time. We can only help you if you act now."

James refused to be backed into a corner. "Call me back in twelve hours and I'll let you know my decision."

"That might be too late."

"I'm willing to take my chances. Good-bye, Mr....shall I say...VEVAK?"

He heard the man draw a sharp breath before James hung up on him.

James drummed his fingers on the table. "Nguyen...we need to talk."

Nguyen cocked his bald head. "How did you know his name was Vevak?"

"If you're going to continue doing business with me, you need to do more reading. There are a lot of organizations with agents lurking in the shadows, agents who could cause us trouble, cause our imprisonment, cause our death." James paused and stared at Nguyen with a deep frown. "VEVAK was a guess on my part. Evidently, a correct guess from the man's reaction. VEVAK, VAJA, MOIS, they're all the same bunch, the intelligence arm of the Iranian government. There are enough rogues among them that I would classify them as a bunch of terrorists."

Nguyen cocked his frowning head. "What made you suspect VEVAK?"

Nguyen was testing his patience. "I'm going to help you understand what's going down here. But keep in mind that I expect you to deduce these things on your own and, in the future, report them to me. No more surprises. Do I make myself clear?"

"Perfectly clear, Mr. James." Nguyen's eyes stared blankly, the look of confusion.

Clear like mud, you ignoramus. "Nguyen, why did we stop using the Internet to coordinate our business? Why was Trader running his own cell service on the Olympic Peninsula?"

"It was becoming too easy for certain organizations to track us." Nguyen gave a wide grin with his answer.

"And how did that sad state of affairs come about?" James waited.

No answer from Nguyen.

"Wasn't it because of the work of a handful of brilliant people, like Jennifer Akihara, that collaboration over the Internet became much easier to detect? Before you answer that, Nguyen, tell me what Jennifer Akihara was working on when she detected the operation on the Olympic Peninsula?"

"I'm not sure. Something about cell-phone communication?" The shar-pei look returned.

"If you had been following all of the news after she broke up the operation in the Northwest like I told you to do, you would have known that she was working on cellular- and wireless-intercept analysis, preparing to do the same thing with wireless communications that she had done with the Internet. It seems those who support terrorists don't want the communication mechanism they are now using to be compromised. They view taking Miss Akihara—now Mrs. Brandt—as a preemptive strike."

"I see." Nguyen's eyes widened. "Iran, VEVAK, Miss Akihara, terrorists funded by Iran—it makes sense. But why didn't they take her before this? And some place where it would be easier to—"

"Why do you suppose, you..." James paused before the insult left his lips. Nguyen was dense, but James still needed the man's cooperation. "No one knew what she was doing until the story about her rescuing the abducted girls hit the media. The news media leaked the information, like they always do. That's why I subscribe to several online newspapers, and it's why I search them every day, as you should also be doing."

Nguyen nodded then frowned again. "What are you going to do about the five-million-dollar offer?"

"Either way, these Iranians are bad news, and I refuse to trust them. You know what the prince will do if we sell to another something he wants badly—something we promised him?"

The shar-pei frown returned.

"That's right, Nguyen. So what do you suppose I'm going to do? Would you cross the prince?"

"No." Nguyen shook his wrinkled brow. "He would kill us like—"

"Like he has several others who have crossed him. I will turn down the Iranian's offer. Hopefully, they will go away. With all of the government scrutiny of events on this island, perhaps the VEVAK will slither out of the heat and back under their rock, never to be seen by us again."

Nguyen was tapping his index finger on the table

to a slow steady rhythm. "When are you planning to tell the VEVAK agent of your decision?"

James smiled. "I'm not going to tell them, Nguyen. *You* are. Now."

Nguyen's finger stopped tapping. His hand balled into a tight fist, then opened. Slowly, he reached for his cell phone.

16

Katie unfolded the map of Kihei in her lap and traced their route to the house as Granddad pulled out from Kukui Mall and headed north. "In about a mile we turn right onto Kauhaa Street. The house is in a residential area south of Kauhaa."

Granddad glanced her way. His look was warm, caring. "I promised Lee I would keep you safe, but I know how much you want to help find Jennifer. As he stipulated, you must stay in the car, but I'll try to park where you can see what is happening."

Katie studied Granddad's kind face. In the few weeks she had known him, he had become her confidant, her mentor in karate as well as in other areas of her life. "Thanks for thinking of me, Granddad. I love you."

It felt awkward to say it. Perhaps because it was the first time she had expressed her feelings so openly towards him. But it was true, so very true. He was like Jennifer...well, a male version. Maybe that's why she grew to love this man so quickly.

A grin spread across his face. "I love you too, Katie girl. Here's Kauhaa. Where is our next turn?"

"Take the second right, onto Laumakani Loop. Then we start looking for a tan house with a lot of vegetation around it. So, what story are you going to tell them?"

Granddad shot her a glance. "I'm looking for my

nephew who used to live at their address, and I thought the people living there might know where he moved to."

"You don't look like you're seventy-two years old. More like fifty. Maybe you should say you're looking for your estranged brother or sister. Be sure not to use your last name, because—"

"Katie, you might beat me at chess almost every game, but your granddad is no fool."

"I'm sorry. That's not what I meant. I just want so badly for this to work—to find Jenn."

"I know. So do I. And we will, Katie. We most certainly will."

When they turned onto the loop, Katie noticed that most of the driveways were lined with small palm trees and flowering bushes. With a little luck, they would be able to park near the house and still keep her hidden from anyone who might be standing at the front door.

Granddad pointed ahead to their left. "That must be the tan house. I'll drive by to—"

She grabbed his arm. "Granddad, stop. Now."

He hit the brakes and pulled to the curb on the left side of the street, leaving a cluster of short palm trees between the car and the house. "What is it, Katie?"

"That's Anya ahead of us, walking towards the house."

"Maybe you should slide down in the seat. We can't let her see you...yet."

"But we need to stop her before she gets into the house."

"I've got it all under control. You just stay out of sight, young lady. "

Katie opened her window as she slid down in her

seat but kept an ear near the window and an eye on the scene unfolding in front of her.

Granddad stepped from the car when Anya turned from the sidewalk onto the walkway leading to the house. "Miss, can you please help me find someone?"

Anya looked back at Granddad as he approached, but then frowned and stepped quickly towards the door. She twisted the doorknob. The door didn't open.

From her vantage point, Katie could still see them through gaps in the trees, and she could hear their conversation.

"My brother used to live in this house. I was hoping someone here might be able to tell me where he moved."

Katie smiled. Granddad had taken her suggestion.

Anya turned a cold shoulder to him and tried to open the door a second time.

Seeing Anya again, Katie could feel Anya's hands yanking her towards the van where other powerful arms had pulled Katie into a nightmare. At recalling those traumatic events, Katie's feelings quickly mushroomed into rage at the thought of this girl doing that to Jennifer.

Before she realized it, she was out of the car, running towards the house. She kept the trees between her and Anya until she reached a point near the house.

Anya turned towards Granddad. "I'm sorry. I can't help you. I think you should leave now."

Anya's back was towards her. Katie slipped through the trees and approached Anya. "You mean you *won't* help him."

Anya turned and gasped. "Katie!" Her eyes widened and she shrank back from Katie who was five inches taller than her and known at school for being exceptionally strong.

"Katie." Granddad's voice grew stern. "Go back to the car now."

Instead Katie stepped closer. "You helped them take me and you helped take Jenn. You won't take anyone again, ever." Katie drove the heel of her left hand into Anya's forehead, snapping her head back and exposing her throat. Katie's right-hand was already balled into a fist, with her knuckles protruding. She swung her hand up in an arc that would deliver a crushing blow to Anya's larynx.

Katie released the jab with all her strength, but an iron vice clamped on her wrist, stopping the jab before it gained its full power.

"Katie! I taught you karate for defense, not to kill. You have shamed me."

Anya rubbed her head and the back of her neck, staring at the two people in front of her.

Granddad's face looked horrible, like someone in pain.

It tore her heart to shreds.

"And if you had killed Anya, how would that have helped Jennifer?"

Katie eyes brimmed with tears. Without Granddad's intervention, she would have killed the girl standing in front of her. *How could I have done that?* It would have been stupid. It would have been wrong.

Anya's eyes widened still farther, revealing a growing horror. "You mean she actually might have killed me?"

"No." Granddad's gaze bored into Anya. "She most certainly would have killed you, and your death would not have been pleasant." He looked at Katie.

"Now you have two people to ask forgiveness from. Then you and I will talk about this."

Katie choked back a sob. "Anya," she reached for Anya, but the girl jumped backward, banging into the door. "Anya, I won't hurt you. Please forgive me. I don't know how—"

"You two are crazy." Anya shook her head, frowning as her gaze darted from Katie to Granddad. "You try to kill me, and then you want me to forgive you? What are you doing here? Don't bother explaining. I'm out of here." She turned to step by Katie, but Granddad's arm shot out and his hand clamped on the top of her shoulder.

When the muscles in his arm flexed, Anya yelped and grimaced, but she stopped moving.

"Be still and I will not hurt you." Granddad spoke in a menacing tone Katie had never heard him use. "But you will tell us about my granddaughter, Jennifer. If you don't, I am tempted to let Katie do whatever she chooses to you."

"No. You don't have to do that. I'll—"

"No more." Granddad's voice had grown as cold as ice, giving Katie a chill just to hear it. "No more delays. Answer my questions. First, who is in the house?"

"No one. I'm locked out. I think everyone left."

His icy voice and stare assaulted Anya again. "Where is Jennifer?" He squeezed her shoulder.

Katie winced when Anya's face contorted in pain. Granddad had demonstrated that painful pressure point to her.

"I don't want to hurt you, Anya. But you must answer me now."

When Katie's composure returned, she realized

that this cool nineteen-year-old girl she had first met at school, a girl who could pass for fifteen, wasn't so cool after all. She looked vulnerable, helpless, even pitiful.

Maybe Anya didn't want to do the things she had been doing.

Where had that thought come from? Katie's emotions rebelled at this suggestion. Realizing Anya obviously had chances to escape while attending school with her, Katie's anger threatened to explode again. She stared at Anya and her gaze traced the tight lines on Anya's face and saw the horror reflected in her eyes. Compassion for this wayward girl melted Katie's anger.

"They took her." Anya's voice was soft. She stared at the ground, avoiding eye contact.

"When?" Granddad's voice grew even colder.

"Please don't do that again." There was complete resignation in her face and voice. "I'll tell you everything I know."

"Then do it now."

Anya took a deep breath then blew it back out. "I walked to the coffee shop on Piikea. It was early, about 6:00 AM. They must've taken her while I was gone." Anya's tone suddenly grew caustic. "They didn't even bother with me. I guess they planned to abandon me or send someone back to deal with me later. You know, something like you started to do, Katie."

Granddad's voice maintained its threatening timbre. "Where did they take Jennifer?"

"They didn't tell me all their plans." She turned her empty hands palms up.

Granddad's gaze bored into Anya's eyes. "But they did have her at this house early this morning?"

"Yes. They held her here since yesterday evening."

"Anya," Katie's voice had a sharp edge on it, "I won't kill you, but Jennifer's life is at stake, so we will use extreme measures. Do we need to start using them now?"

"No. But if I tell you anything more, they'll kill me. They'll probably kill me for what I've already said. It doesn't matter where I go, they'll track me down and kill me, and it won't be pleasant. Not the way they'll do it."

Katie had tried to hang onto the anger she felt towards Anya, but the girl's vulnerability and a growing realization of the depravity of the men who controlled her had eroded it away leaving only pity.

Anya's gaze again darted from Katie's face to Granddad's. "They...they talked about moving her to a boat. Not in a harbor. I think it was a yacht anchored somewhere on this side of the island."

"Whose yacht?" Granddad demanded.

"That's all I know."

Air blasted from Granddad's lungs. "And why should we believe you?"

"Because...I think Katie will kill me if I don't tell you everything I know."

Katie studied Anya's eyes. There was anxiety, but at least she met their gaze. "She's telling the truth, Granddad."

Granddad stepped close to the frightened girl.

Anya shrank back.

He stopped his advance and gave her his penetrating stare. "One more question, Anya. Was Jennifer harmed in any way?"

Anya shook her head. "She was tied with restraints. They're not comfortable, and they drugged her once to make her sleep for a while, but she looked all right when she woke up. I think Jennifer will be safe...well, until they sell her."

Katie stepped toe-to-toe with Anya. "When do they plan to sell her?"

She tried to read Anya's face. Was that sadness? Maybe Anya was putting on some kind of act like when she pretended to befriend Katie at school. "Anya, when do they plan to sell Jenn?"

"The Amber Alert has caused a lot of problems. I heard them say they'd sell her as soon as they got a chance."

17

Katie studied Anya's face, trying to read her heart. Katie's Bible said reading people's hearts was God's domain, but she had to try. There were questions she wanted to ask this girl. Dozens of them. Like, how could she help these men capture girls?

Granddad's cell rang. "It's Lee. Katie, I'm turning on the speakerphone so you can hear."

"Granddad, I'm on my way over to meet you. There was no one at the house in south Kihei. What did you and Katie find?"

"We found Katie's, uh, friend, Anya."

"Anya? What about Jennifer?" Lee's voice rose.

"They moved her, Lee."

Silence.

"Where?"

"You need to come over here. When you get here, we will fill you in. The house is the fourth or fifth on the left side of Laumakani Loop. We have...detained Anya, and she may be willing to cooperate, so it's time to call the police."

"I should be there in two or three minutes. Then I'll call Detective Ramirez."

After Granddad closed his cell, Anya stared at the ground and shuffled her feet. In a few moments, she looked up at Katie. "He's going to call the police when he gets here. I wonder what they'll do with me?"

"It depends," Katie said, once again studying the

face of this girl who helped human traffickers. "It depends on *why* you help them. How can you do that, Anya? Destroy another girl's life for..." She couldn't verbalize that cruel, perverted reality.

Katie's question appeared to strike Anya like a blow. She looked away from Katie and clenched her jaw. "I have to do whatever they want...anything."

Katie glared at Anya. "That's not true! You had chances to escape while you were at my school. You could have told the—"

"No! You don't understand!" Anya's face contorted in terror. "The things they would do to me if—" Anya shuddered. After her gaze dropped to the ground, her voice softened. "Helping them was better than what they made me do at first. You don't have a clue what it's like to be...to be sold...over and over and over again—" Anya choked back a sob. Tears overflowed her eyes and spilled onto her cheeks.

Could she trust Anya, or was this another act like when she pretended to be her friend at school, before helping those goons kidnap her? Katie's mind said, "Don't trust her." But her heart pulled her in another direction.

As the events Anya described played out in her mind like a scene in a movie, the painful wrenching of Katie's heart erased the final traces of anger. She looked into Anya's tear-filled eyes and saw a girl that she might have become had Jennifer and Lee not risked their lives to save her. Katie reached out for Anya. This time the girl fell into her arms.

"It doesn't matter anymore." Anya spoke between sobs. "They'll kill me anyway. I'll talk to the police."

Granddad opened his mouth, studied Katie's face, closed it again, and stepped away from the two girls.

"They won't be able to hurt you anymore. The police can help you, Anya. We can help you. I know the FBI agent in charge of the investigation. But best of all, God can help you." Katie couldn't believe she'd said that. One moment, she was ready to kill this girl. The next, she wanted to introduce her to God. *Please, Lord, forgive me for...You know...for all of it.*

Anya pulled her head back, glanced at Katie's face, and dropped her gaze to the ground. "After all I've done, God probably wants me dead, too."

Katie couldn't let their conversation end on that sour note. "No. That's not what God wants." She paused, waiting for Anya to respond.

Silence. No eye contact.

"Please, Anya, look at me. This is important."

Anya wiped her cheeks and slowly raised her gaze to meet Katie's.

Katie tried to give her a warm smile. "As soon as we get a chance to talk, I've got some really good news to share with you."

18

Lee braked hard as he pulled to the curb beside Granddad's rented car.

Granddad stood in the yard looking his way. A few feet behind him, Katie had her arms around a shorter, blonde girl. Anya? This wasn't what he expected to see.

Lee jumped from his car and headed towards the three people standing near the front door of the house. His anger surged out of control. Anya had helped the traffickers abduct Katie several weeks ago and then helped them take Jennifer. How could a teenage girl be so callous and cruel? He strode towards Anya, wondering what her neck would feel like in his hands as he wrung it.

When Lee approached the three, Granddad stepped in front of him, blocking his path and gripping his shoulders with hands like vise clamps. "Lee, no! Anya is going to help us. I think she's been through enough already…perhaps too much."

Lee took a calming breath and another look at Katie who was still comforting the girl he could now see had been crying. His gaze alternated between Granddad and Katie. "What's going on here?"

"Don't take your frustrations out on Anya. She has agreed to cooperate with the police." Granddad released Lee's shoulders.

"What about cooperating with us?" Lee shot Anya

a searing glance.

"Lee, she has already done that. She told us that early this morning they moved Jennifer from the house to a yacht anchored somewhere on the west side of the island. We also know they plan to sell her as soon as possible."

Lee shook his head. "That's not much for us to go on."

"But it's all she knows." Granddad drew Lee's gaze. "I'm sure of it, because I...shall we say, got her attention. So did Katie."

So it was OK for Granddad to use his karate on her but not for Lee to wring her neck. *Wringing her neck is a little more permanent.* Lee stepped towards Anya again.

Granddad pulled him back. "Anya was taken, abducted just like Katie. But no one rescued her. She was forced into a life she did not choose, forced to make choices she would never have made under normal circumstances."

When he looked at Anya again, he no longer saw a hardened, nineteen-year-old woman. Instead she was a fifteen-year-old girl like Katie...beautiful, innocent, and unspoiled. The innocent girl quickly morphed to a young woman with tear-stained cheeks. Realizing what had happened to Anya drove a knife into his gut. He winced when the message Granddad conveyed twisted the knife.

He took a deep breath, blew it all out in a sharp blast, and patted Granddad's shoulder. "I'm OK now."

Lee moved towards Anya, but she cowered behind Katie.

He stopped when he recognized the deep fear in her eyes. "Anya, if you're going to cooperate with the police to help them find Jennifer, I'm on your side. I know the FBI agent in charge, so I can plead your case with him."

Anya slipped from behind Katie and faced him. "No matter what you or anyone else tries to do, they'll still kill me."

He heard the resignation in her voice. It was a voice devoid of hope, the one thing no human being can live long without. Maybe he could remedy that. "Have you heard of the Witness Protection Program?"

Anya nodded. "I've heard of it. But it doesn't matter where anyone hides me. These people kill everyone who crosses them. They'll track me down and kill me, and what they do is a lot worse than just killing people."

Lee stepped close and laid a hand on her shoulder.

Anya flinched.

He didn't remove his hand. "Don't worry, Anya." He wiped a tear from her cheek, then circled both Katie and Anya with his arms. "I can't promise you the Witness Protection Program. Only the Department of Justice can do that. But I do know this, no one in that program has ever been lost if they stayed in it. Not even the most powerful members of the Mafia have been able to find them. If they offer you that protection, Anya, you *will* be safe."

Lee stepped back from their huddle and studied Anya's face. She still wore a wary look. Doubt filled her eyes, but he also saw a glimmer of hope. Evidently he had told her something she wanted to believe. Maybe it was a place for her to begin—to begin building hope and begin rebuilding her life. He prayed the law enforcement officers involved would help her in that process.

Lee turned to Granddad and pulled out his cell. "I

think Anya's ready. It's time to call the police, and I'm going to start with Peterson instead of detective Ramirez. He might be a little more receptive to what I've got to say."

Katie's voice came from behind him. "You better be careful, Lee. I've seen you two tangle before. What's Peterson going to think about us doing *his* work?"

"We're about to find out, Katie." Lee hit Peterson's number on his speed dial.

"Betcha five dollars he uses his one cuss word." Katie grinned at him.

"Actually Peterson knows two words." Lee returned the grin. "But you don't want to hear the second one."

Peterson answered on the fifth ring. He must've been busy.

"Brandt, I've got a multi-organizational task force to operate. This had better be important or—"

"Peterson, we caught Anya, one of the perps."

"You did what?" His voice crescendoed and, from experience, Lee knew this was the calm before the storm.

"Blast it, Lee! You might have disrupted a SWAT team in—"

"But I didn't, did I?"

"Blast it all to blazes! Do I have to lock you up to keep you from interfering?"

"You know I didn't interfere, Peterson. You told me you were coming at this investigation from another angle, so don't you tell me—"

Peterson exhausted his meager cursing vocabulary in a two-word song played entirely in fortissimo.

Lee jerked the cell away from his head to save his eardrums.

"We could hear that clear over here," Katie said. "Like I told you, Lee, You'd better be careful."

Peterson's voice dropped a few decibels. "I have half a mind to lock you up for—"

"Peterson, if you aren't interested in what we learned from Anya, half a mind is about all you've got."

"That's it!" Peterson boomed out using his voice of authority. "You're under arrest for—"

"Since you're not present to arrest me, you'll have to catch me first. Is that how you want to use your resources right now?"

Peterson muttered something incoherent, and then his end of the conversation fell silent.

Lee waited.

A deep sigh came from Peterson's end. "I'm in my car in Maalaea. Where are *you*?"

"Katie, Jennifer's grandfather, and I are with Anya at a house on the north side of Kihei. Anya wants to cooperate, and I think she's got a lot to tell us." Lee pled Anya's case like he had promised and then gave the FBI agent the address of the suspects' house.

"I'm on my way. I'll see you in about fifteen minutes." Peterson's voice sounded like he had cooled down a bit. "Get in your cars and be prepared to leave if any vehicle other than a police car approaches. I'll call Ramirez while I'm en route."

Less volume. No more expletives. No further mention of arresting him. Those were all good signs. "We'll wait right here unless the goons return."

"Don't worry about them. I just sent a patrol car to the house. It's coming from the Piilani Village Shopping Center. You should hear a siren shortly."

"Yeah. I hear him," Lee replied.

When Peterson ended the call, flashing lights raced down the east end of Laumakani Loop. He closed his cell and moved beside Anya. "Don't worry." He gestured towards the approaching police car. "These guys are your best friends right now. They might ask a lot of questions, but they'll also keep you safe."

Anya's face tilted downward. "I haven't had a friend—haven't deserved one—in a long time."

Katie drew Anya's gaze. "Maybe that's about to change." She gave Anya a thin-lipped smile. "I'd like to be your friend, if you'll let me."

"I still think you guys are crazy."

The patrol car pulled to the curb in front of the house and both front doors flew open.

Granddad walked out to meet the two officers approaching slowly, as if ready to pull their guns.

Katie took Anya's hand. "I'm right beside you, girl. And when we get a chance, I've still got some good news to tell you."

As Lee watched Katie, he was conflicted. He was proud of her, but until Jennifer was safely in his arms again, his heart was too sick to share its feelings.

19

On the rear deck of his yacht, Franklin James moved his chair out of the hot sun and rested his hand on the table. His fingers tapped a syncopated rhythm. He was nervous...no, concerned. Franklin James was too careful and intelligent to be nervous.

Mrs. Brandt, for practical purposes, still Miss Akihara, had been aboard his yacht for nearly two hours. The search by the authorities would only intensify. Sometime within the next twelve hours their scrutiny would probably reach his yacht.

He drew a breath and pounded a fist into the table. "Snake."

The clomping of running feet sounded shortly before Snake's tall, slender form rounded the starboard corner of the yacht. "Yes, Mr. James?"

"Have you seen any indications that we are under surveillance?"

"Not until a couple of minutes ago. I was just about to—"

"You should have told me immediately." *I can't even trust my most loyal employee.*

"I planned to. But when you called, I had my binoculars on them, trying to identify them."

"Them? How many were there, and from where are they watching?" His fingers drummed the table at a furious pace.

"I think it's two of our Iranian friends. They were

dressed like tourists, in shorts and T-shirts, standing on the trail at Wailea Point watching us with binoculars."

"How do you know they're *not* tourists?"

"My high-powered binocs. And they've been watching us for five minutes straight, probably longer. And they look Middle Eastern."

"You didn't let them—"

"No, Mr. James." Snake shook his head. "They didn't see me watching them. I made sure I was well hidden."

"They're still after our cargo. Sounds like our rich customers would rather become thieves. They won't try anything before tonight and by then"—he smiled—"our million-dollar girl will be gone. But if they don't know that, they might still attack so we need to—"

His cell rang. "We'll continue our discussion after this call." He answered with an anonymous hello.

"It's Mack. I went back to the house to do what you told me."

"Did you take care of the girl?"

"I couldn't even approach the place. It was surrounded by the entire MPD."

"What about the girl?"

"They have her. I could see that much."

"But she was never informed of our plans. How big of a problem can a teenager be?"

Mack was silent for a few moments. "We shouldn't underestimate her. Anya is smart. Really smart. If she overheard even a few words of our plans, she would figure them out soon enough."

James sighed. "The MPD will help in that process. We can be sure of that." He paused. "Come on back. Forget the girl." He ended the call.

They would have to cut their losses and be

prepared to leave paradise before it turned into hades. Paradise lost? Soon. Probably very soon. *But hopefully he could salvage the million dollars.*

"Snake, contact our intermediary. Let the prince know he has three hours to claim his merchandise or it gets dumped into the water. And he needs to let me know, in advance, how he plans to rendezvous, or the deal is off. Don't worry. He'll understand why the plans are changing."

"I'm on it, Mr. James." Snake whirled and disappeared around the corner on the port side of the yacht.

****

Jennifer lay on the floor of the cabin drenched with her efforts to free her hands. Burning, throbbing pain radiated from both wrists bound behind her. Warm fluid made the nylon restraints sticky. Her wrists were bleeding, and still she'd made no progress with the restraints on her wrists or her ankles.

Her salty perspiration had seeped under the edge of the duct tape covering her mouth. It made her raw lips and patches of irritated skin on her cheeks sting, bringing tears to her eyes.

Unless she developed a new plan, she would never escape. With that realization, she factored risk out of the equation as she sought a new approach.

Footsteps sounded outside the window of the cabin. Was someone about to enter?

Other footsteps came from the opposite direction. When the footsteps stopped, she heard the muffled sounds of voices. Jennifer strained to understand the words.

"…forget the girl…" The voice was Cookie's.

"The prince has three hours," Snake's hiss said, "then we bail."

The voices stopped and footsteps sounded again, growing faint as the two men walked away from the door.

If they planned to sell her to the prince as they mentioned once before, she had less than three hours to escape. If the prince got his filthy hands on her, she would have to—she couldn't let that happen. If James and his men bailed, they would kill her. Of that she was certain.

This isn't working. Please God, show me something else to try.

20

Like a wild animal in a zoo, Lee paced back and forth on the sidewalk outside the house near Granddad and Katie. On his fifth pass, Peterson's car rolled to a stop on Laumakani Loop. He was much later than he said. More time wasted, precious time.

Since Lee had talked with the FBI agent, more Maui police officers had arrived, including the crime-scene technicians who were conferring with Anya. Detective Ramirez had finally arrived, and he took the last available parking spot within a block of the house.

Peterson's window was down. Lee locked gazes with him. "Good luck finding a parking place."

After parking, Peterson sought out Ramirez. The two talked for a couple of minutes. Precious minutes.

Katie and Granddad joined Lee on the sidewalk.

When the tall FBI agent finally approached them, Lee confronted him. "Peterson, Anya told us the goons took Jennifer to some yacht before sunrise this morning. What are you doing to find it?"

Peterson stopped, hands on hips. "We have a lot of leads, Lee. And we're pursuing the most promising ones."

"But this lead is—

"Listen for a second, because that's about all I've got right now. We think one of the leaders of the trafficking ring is on the island. If we find him, we'll find Jennifer."

If Peterson insisted on that approach instead of looking for a yacht, either he was holding back information or he had another agenda, one that didn't place Jennifer's safety as the highest priority. At that thought, Lee's emotions became a vial of smoking nitro. "Are you sure about that? Do you realize what happens if you're wrong?"

"All right, if it will get you to shut up." Peterson stared sequentially at Lee, Katie and Granddad. "We've assembled information from the Coast Guard, our field agents, Interpol and the FBI's intelligence group. It tells us the big boss is on the island. He is the one who would capture Jennifer to make a statement. That's how we know." He paused. "I can't tell you any more than that, Lee. You'll have to trust that we know what we're doing."

Lee returned Peterson's stare. "Then you'll have to trust that I know what I'm doing."

Peterson pulled a hand from his hip and poked his index finger into Lee's chest. "If you pull any more stunts like you and Jennifer did at Rialto Beach, I'll have you arrested."

Lee knocked the tall FBI agent's hand away. Lee was on the verge of an explosion and he really didn't care. "The little stunt you're referring to saved three girls' lives and wiped out most of the trafficking ring...without any help from you and your snail-paced response."

Katie wedged her body between the two men. "I talked with Anya, Peterson. She's a victim, too. And the men in the organization will kill her for what she's already told us. Is there any way you can keep her safe?"

Katie had changed the subject. She had pried the

two men apart, and she had probably saved him from doing something he would've regretted. What was he thinking? One didn't assault an FBI agent, especially a good man like Peterson. Lee stepped back out of his reach.

Peterson reciprocated, pulling his hands back into his own personal space. He focused on Katie. "We still have a few missing pieces to our trafficking-ring puzzle. If Anya cooperates and supplies them, maybe I can help her. But I can't promise her Witness Protection. That's a DOJ call made by people higher up than me. "

A Maui police officer emerged from the house leading Anya.

Peterson turned towards the officer. "I'm Special Agent Peterson, and I'd like a word with Anya."

As Peterson talked to Anya, Lee stood nearby listening and hoping something productive would come out of their conversation.

Peterson introduced himself and skillfully opened the door for Anya to cooperate with the FBI. "Did the police tell you that you don't have to answer any questions?"

"They explained that, but I want to answer."

"You've made a wise decision, Anya. If you help us break the syndicate, I'll do everything I can to help you."

Anya stared into the distance as if seeing everything, yet seeing nothing. "Nobody can help me once they come after me."

"You shouldn't think that way. They've instilled a deep-seated fear in you. But these men aren't invincible. We'll get them. Then you'll see that you don't need to live in fear of them." He paused and reached into his pocket, pulling out his cell. "But I want to ask you about some other people."

Peterson pulled a picture up on his cell and turned the display towards Anya.

Lee stepped closer to peer around his shoulder.

"Have you seen either of these men in the last twenty-four hours?"

Anya drew in a sharp breath. She didn't reply. Fear lurked in her wide eyes.

Lee also saw the picture of two Middle Eastern looking men. *The Iranian connection?*

Peterson moved the picture closer to Anya. "This is extremely important. These men may ask questions about Jennifer. If you have any information, anything at all, it will certainly help your cause if you tell me now."

Anya stared at the picture. Her mouth twitched, then slowly opened. "These men...aren't just evil. They're crazy."

Peterson's body flinched at Anya's words, like she had struck him. "Then you *have* seen them. When? Where?"

"They said *they* would kill me too if I mentioned them to anyone. But I guess they'll have to get in line." She looked up into Peterson's face and gave him a smile that contained more pain than anything else. "When I left the house early this morning to walk to the coffee shop at Piilani Center, they stopped me a couple blocks from the house. Began asking questions about a woman. Asked for the name of the person who owned her. I knew they were asking about Jennifer."

Peterson held Anya's gaze. "But you said Jennifer was still at the house when you left."

"She was." Anya's face for the first time displayed

a softer, more compassionate look. "Like I said, these guys were completely insane. You wouldn't believe some of the things they threatened to do. I told them Jennifer had been moved to a boat."

Anya had lied to protect Jennifer. It was a small thing, given the fact she helped with Jennifer's abduction, but it revealed a young, caring girl hidden somewhere inside this hardened young woman, the girl who existed before the traffickers stole her innocence and terrified her into submission. The good news Katie wanted to share with her was the only thing Lee believed could restore her innocence and provide the healing she needed from the abuses Anya had suffered.

Peterson pulled out his notepad and pen. "What about the name they asked for?"

"I heard a couple of names mentioned at the house, people I'd never met. Men I assumed were leaders in the trafficking ring. I gave the lunatics their names."

Peterson's voice softened. "I need to know the names you gave them, Anya."

Anya shrugged. "I heard them mention a Nguyen and a Mr. James."

Peterson's expression changed at the last name, James. Obviously he knew more about the traffickers than he was telling Lee.

"Thanks, Anya. You've been a big help to me. I won't forget it." He put a hand on her shoulder. "But right now, you need to go with the Maui police. They'll have a lot of questions for you, but consider them your friends because they will keep you safe."

Two Maui police officers approached Anya, and she gave Peterson a weak smile. "That's what Lee said too."

Lee stepped close to her. "Please help the police any way you can. Your cooperation could save Jennifer's life."

"Remember what I said about the good news?" Katie called out as the police led Anya away. "I'll see you soon, and we can talk about it."

Anya turned towards Katie, opened her mouth, then closed it and turned to face the Maui policemen.

Lee's gaze bored into Peterson. "The two men in the pictures you showed to Anya...they're the Iranian connection."

Peterson finished writing in his notepad and looked up at Lee. "That didn't sound like a question."

Lee stared back at him, his patience now gone. "It wasn't. They're part of the...what is it the Iranians call their intelligence organization?"

Peterson sighed. "Ministry of Intelligence and National Security. Sometimes called by acronyms like VEVAK or VAJA. Parts of the organization have secret operating budgets, and there are rogue elements among the agents. That makes it hard to know who's doing what, for whom, and why."

Lee shifted his weight from side to side as the antsiness of uncertainty moved his feet and cramped in his stomach. "You're not very encouraging. That's the group that committed the chain murders back in the '90s, isn't it?"

"Yes. But—"

"And these are the guys who want Jennifer." Lee sensed he was on the verge of losing his composure again.

"Lee,"—Peterson studied his face—"they don't have Jennifer, and they're not going to get her."

Katie stepped beside Lee.

Lee glared at the tall FBI agent. "That's the only reason you came, isn't it? Because of the national security risks." He had given Peterson a cruel stab from his poison tongue, and Lee wanted the words back as soon as he spat them out.

"No, it wasn't the only reason. But it did provide justification for us to—"

"If you aren't going to find her, we will." Katie's words were another stab, a low blow.

Peterson pursed his lips and dropped his gaze to the ground.

Lee pulled Katie close to his side and looked up at the tall man. "I'm...we're sorry. We had no reason to accuse you. But we can't sit idly by while Jennifer's being held by a bunch of depraved demoniacs."

"Like I said, don't do what you did at Rialto Beach." Peterson stared into Lee's eyes with his frowning face of authority. "You nearly got yourselves killed. I'm going back to the police station at Wailuku to be there when they interrogate Anya. I'll be in touch."

The fluttering feelings of panic crawled through Lee's stomach. Things were moving far too slowly. He had wasted far too much time at the house and no one, Peterson included, seemed to be in a hurry to act on the latest information.

He turned towards Granddad. "Obviously Peterson thinks his top-down approach is the best way to find Jennifer. What do you think?"

"Let the FBI search for the big kahuna. We need to search the west side of the island for an anchored yacht."

"My thoughts exactly," Lee said. "But the whales

have already begun arriving, so now we have hundreds of boats in the water, including quite a few yachts."

"We think it is anchored. But beyond that…" Granddad gave a palms-up shrug.

Katie's gaze darted from Lee to Granddad and back again. "While I was talking to her, Anya said the goons never mentioned another female other than her. That means—"

"That we're looking for a yacht with no women visible on board," Lee said. "It's anchored, not moving. And since the search for Jennifer is intensifying, these goons are going to be vigilant, looking for anyone who's looking at them." Lee's mind seemed to be on a roll. "So if we're not too obvious, we can let them see us looking at them. It may evoke a telltale response." He paused. "We can pick up binoculars for all of us at the Pacific Whale Foundation store in Maalaea. Then…"

Katie frowned at him. "Don't stop now, Lee. You were doing great."

The fluttering in his stomach returned. "Let's drive to Maalaea. Then we'll need to split up to cover as much of the area as possible, but I'm not sure where we should concentrate our search."

Granddad laid a hand on his shoulder. "There are only two areas where we are likely to see an anchored yacht on the west side of Maui."

Granddad's words yanked Lee's gaze to the elderly man's face.

"What two areas?"

"The first area is from Lahaina northward to the resort hotels, and the second is from Maalaea Bay south to Makena." Granddad sighed. "Since I know the island better than you, let me take the area from Lahaina northward. I will take Katie with me because we have more territory to cover."

He continued, "Lee, if you buy the most powerful binoculars they sell at the store, you can cover the entire area using only two observations points. I would suggest Waipuilani Park in Kihei, and then Wailea Point. The point is on the beach trail a little south of the Grand Wailea Resort. Katie, will you please get the map from our car. The one we used to navigate to this house."

When Katie returned with the map, Granddad marked the two observation points for Lee. "Check Maalaea Bay from Waipuilani Park first. You might be able to eliminate it quickly because boats usually move through the bay rather than anchor there. Then move to Wailea Point. You can see most of your area from the point, so that's where I would spend most of my time."

"Thanks, Granddad. Let's head for Maalaea. And for the rest of the day, forget about the island speed limits. Let's keep in mind the two names Anya mentioned, James and Nguyen." He paused. "I think we need to come up with a suspicious yacht within the next two hours. If not, I'm afraid we may be too late."

21

"Snake." James sighed as the slender man appeared. "Get the prince on the secure phone. I need to know where he is, when he's arriving, and how he wants to transfer the merchandise."

"Sure thing, Mr. James. Give me a couple of minutes to get him on the line." Snake disappeared around the starboard corner of the yacht.

One way or another, James wanted the troublesome little beauty off his yacht in thirty minutes or less. Very soon she would become either the prince's problem or shark bait, very expensive shark bait.

Snake returned in a couple minutes with the phone. "He's on the line, he wouldn't give me the info you requested. Said he'll only talk to you."

James reached for the phone and prepared for his performance, a balancing act where rationality and the prince's appetites were brought into equilibrium. An act James hated to perform, but one he'd never yet failed at. Those who failed...most were no longer around.

He put the receiver to his ear. "This is James."

"Mr. James, I would like to conclude our business matter as soon as possible." The prince's voice was more demanding than usual.

"How soon can you get here?" James would gladly hand his problem cargo over to the prince. The sooner the better.

"I will arrive in thirty minutes."

"Thirty minutes will be fine."

"Which side of your vessel is toward the shore?"

So the prince was worried. Worried, but not deterred from claiming his coveted prize, the woman he said was the most beautiful he had ever seen. "The port side."

"See that you hold that position. I will come alongside, and the cargo will be discreetly loaded from your port side onto my vessel."

"Rest assured the cargo will be accessible from the port side."

"There shall be no visibility of the cargo from the shore anywhere from Maalaea to Makena." The prince's voice became more demanding.

"That's quite a stretch of shoreline. But I will ensure that the transfer is not visible from the shore. You do have the payment we agreed upon?"

Silence.

"You felt the need to ask? You are breaking my heart, Mr. James. How long have we been doing business?"

"This is a...much larger and more delicate transaction than normal, and I have immediate travel plans, so—"

"Be ready in thirty minutes. If you do not appear to be ready—if anything does not appear ready—consider the transaction cancelled, because I will also have travel plans."

"I will be ready. Thirty minutes."

James terminated the call and looked up at his most trusted employee. "Only one small wrinkle, Snake. We need to move the cargo to a room on the port side."

"I'm on it, boss." Snake hissed. "About the move—"

"Just make sure no one sees her. Put her in the guest bedroom and check it to make sure there are no sharp objects lying around. Our previous guest smoked. We don't want any matches or lighters in there either."

****

Footsteps outside. The door to the cabin opened. From where Jennifer lay on the floor, she watched the long body of Snake step into the room and close the door behind him.

"It looks like you didn't listen to me," Snake hissed. "You wrists are bleeding again, Snow White."

Jennifer frowned at his new name for her.

"Puzzled, are we? You shouldn't be, Snow White. You always knew that someday your prince would come." Snake expelled a breathy laugh as he rolled her body onto an area rug covering part of the floor.

"We can do this the easy way or the hard way. I'm going to roll you in this carpet and move you to another room. If anyone sees you outside, into the water you go. Mr. James's orders. So I suggest you stretch out like a stick and be very still."

Another room might offer more possibilities for escape. She had found nothing here. And the window of opportunity was rapidly closing.

Jennifer stretched out her legs.

Snake rolled her in the carpet, slung her over his shoulder, and carried her out the door.

The combination of the tape over her mouth and the carpet pressing against her face sent her pulse pounding as panic assaulted her rational mind. Jennifer's rapid breathing through her nose accelerated. Each breath was shorter than the previous one, like the length of unburned fuse trailing from the emotional bomb that would soon send her into a claustrophobic cataclysm.

When she lost it, Snake would drop her on the deck and the carpet would unroll. Her exposure would give James an excuse to drop her in the water. Jennifer exerted a strength of will she didn't know she possessed to defuse the panic attack. She forced her respiration to slow to long, equal breaths. She willfully made her body relax from its rigid state and prayed she could retain enough sanity to endure her confinement in the carpet coffin for a while longer.

Snake stopped. Then came the sound of a door opening. He moved again.

It grew darker inside the carpeting. She smelled stale cigarette smoke.

He dropped her.

She braced for the impact with the floor. Instead her body bounced on a bed and spun around twice as Snake pulled the carpet from her body, nearly rolling her onto the floor.

With her head swimming, Jennifer lay on the bed in a dim room that reeked of cigarette smoke. She sneezed.

"Sorry if I've offended your delicate sensitivities," Snake hissed, "but all of the nonsmoking rooms have been taken."

The awful odor in the room and the sense of evil Snake produced threatened to take whatever was left of her breakfast. Jennifer fought the nausea, not wanting to give him the satisfaction of seeing how much he had disturbed her.

He gripped her upper arms, pulled her onto the floor, and then released her. "Now let's see what we might need to remove from the premises." Snake scanned the room then stopped, his feet beside her head.

Jennifer followed his gaze to the wall.

"Mirror, mirror, on the wall... Sorry, Snow White, but your mirror has got to go. Wouldn't want you to hurt yourself before Prince Charming arrives. In about fifteen minutes I get to give you away to him. Nothing fancy, just a simple little ceremony. Then it's off on your honeymoon." Snake laughed a breathy laugh as he pulled the mirror from its wall mounts, carried it out, and closed the door behind him.

Unless Snake was just taunting her, fifteen minutes was all she had if she ever wanted to see Lee again. Jennifer rolled onto her stomach and pushed her forehead into the floor. She needed her hands in front of her to make any progress.

Jennifer pulled her knees under her. She rocked backward into a kneeling position. With hands behind her, she surveyed the room for anything she could use to cut through the restraints. She spotted a heavy ceramic ashtray on a nightstand by the bed.

Footsteps sounded at the door. She prepared herself to roll prostrate on the floor again, but the footsteps stopped. She waited. The feet shuffled occasionally, but the person did not walk away. Evidently she had a guard outside. The guard would complicate things. Now she must worry about making any noises.

I've only got about ten minutes.

She folded her body against her knees, straining to

pull her two hands around her rear to the front side. They wouldn't go. She extended her arms and pulled downward with her wrists using all of her strength. She toppled onto the floor on her side, sweating profusely. It wasn't working.

At this point she would have gladly traded her shapely figure for one of those '60s beanpole models. Once again she felt the sting of sweat around her mouth as she struggled to return to the kneeling position.

Please, Lord, show me how to do this.

Jennifer took a deep breath and tried to relax her entire body while she released all of the air in her lungs. She rocked back and forth, took another breath, and rocked back as the last of it left her lungs.

Her hands slipped around her seat and caught behind her knees. She was almost there.

More footsteps sounded outside. There were voices. No matter, she couldn't stop now. She toppled onto her side, slid the ankles restraints as high as they would go on her wrists, and worked her feet, one at a time, through the restraining bands.

The silhouette of the guard appeared on the curtain covering the cabin window. It didn't move. Maybe he would remain in his spot near the door. But how long would it be until they checked on her again? If they saw her progress, they might drug her.

With the fear of drugs came more adrenaline and more strength.

Standing on her bound feet, Jennifer pulled the tape from her mouth and waddled to the nightstand, where she grabbed the ashtray. It was made of a heavy ceramic material. She waddled to the bathroom door and wrapped one layer of hand towel around the ashtray. She raised it above her head and smashed it onto the corner of the sink.

Only a dull thud. The towel muffled the sound, but it also softened the blow.

Jennifer positioned the ashtray at the precise spot she wanted to strike and carefully raised her hands, like a golfer's backswing, to a position high above her head.

Please help me do this.

Using all of her strength, Jennifer smashed the ashtray onto the sharpest edge of the sink.

22

From Lee's vantage point at Waipuilani Park, he could see that all the vessels were either moving through the bay's shallow blue waters looking for whales or were headed from Maalaea to another destination. Less than twenty minutes after leaving the store at Maalaea, Lee had eliminated Maalaea Bay from consideration.

He left the beach and strode to his car. He pulled out Katie's map and scanned the Wailea area. There was a parking lot with beach access on the southern edge of the Grand Wailea Resort.

He left the park and drove south towards Wailea.

In about ten minutes, he passed the shops at Wailea and then the Grand Wailea Resort. The road turned to the right and climbed a hill. Near the top Lee saw the beach access sign. He turned in and grabbed a parking spot being vacated by an older couple.

After maneuvering into the undersized space, he glanced at his watch. An hour had passed since he told Katie and Granddad they needed to find the yacht. He had only an hour left if they were going to meet the timetable he had set.

Lee grabbed his binoculars and trotted down the path through the park. He climbed over a grassy knoll and stepped onto a paved beach trail about one hundred yards south of the big resort. To his left, about two hundred yards away, volcanic rock jutted out into the water. Wailea Point. He jogged towards it, passing several slow walkers on the trail.

After reaching the point, Lee stepped off the trail onto an undeveloped area evidently used by the more adventuresome tourists to walk down to the lava outcropping at the water's edge. With his naked eye, he scanned the water from south to north. From this vantage point he could easily see from Molikini up to Kihei, his remaining area of responsibility.

Lee raised the binoculars and began a systematic search for anything resembling an anchored yacht.

One vessel large enough to qualify as a yacht was anchored two hundred yards south of Wailea Point, on the northern edge of a popular snorkeling destination called Turtle Town. Several smaller catamarans were anchored there, surrounded by the bobbing heads of snorkelers. It was a good place for a boat to anchor and yet remain relatively inconspicuous among the numerous other boats that stopped for periods of time for snorkeling.

Lee explored the yacht with his binoculars for a few minutes. A man sat at a table on the rear deck. A tall slender man seemed to be at his beck and call. Another man occasionally appeared on deck. He was shorter and stockier. There were three cabins on the visible side of the yacht. Probably three more on the other side.

Did one of them hold Jennifer? He prayed his observations would provide enough clues to answer that question.

On a small point a quarter mile to the south, two men stood looking seaward. They also seemed to be watching the yacht with binoculars. But perhaps they were only watching the snorkelers or turtles.

Lee moved behind a six-foot-high bush lining a portion of the trail and maneuvered into position to watch the two men without being seen by them. When he raised his binoculars for a closer look at them, they were gone.

Lee's cell phone rang.

"Lee, it's Katie. We finished looking around Lahaina and didn't find anything."

"Where are you now, Katie?"

"We're a few miles south of Lahaina, headed your direction. Granddad's driving and he's really got a lead foot. He says to tell you we'll be there in about twenty minutes. Any calls from Peterson or the Maui police?"

"No, nothing." Should he mention the yacht? It was too soon to be certain, but they all needed some encouraging news. "But I may have found the yacht."

"Granddad, Lee thinks he found it." Katie's voice rose in pitch and volume.

"Granddad wants to know where the yacht is anchored."

"Tell him it's a little south of Wailea Point, at the edge of Turtle Town."

Lee waited while Granddad talked with Katie.

"Granddad wants you to meet us at the Kihei boat ramp. He thinks we need to get close to the yacht to check it out and, if we have to, intervene to prevent them from selling Jennifer."

"Getting in close is a good idea. We can't call Peterson with a false alarm. We have to know we've got the right boat when we call, or a lot of bad things could happen. The intervention part...we'll play that by ear." If that scenario started to unfold, he would have Katie removed immediately.

"I turned on the speakerphone," Katie said. "He heard you and agrees. His cousin rents boats at the Kihei ramp and owes Granddad...big time. So he'll have one ready for us by the time we get there."

"Great. I know where the boat ramp is. I'll be there when you two arrive. Tell Granddad he needs to use his lead foot."

"The speedometer says seventy-five, Lee. You should see this road, twisting and winding above the ocean. I don't think—"

"He's got the idea, Katie. I'll see you in a few minutes."

Lee stood beside the boat ramp parking area tapping out a snappy rhythm with his foot when Granddad's rented car turned in. He glanced at his watch. Less than thirty minutes left on Lee's self-imposed two-hour deadline.

They needed a fast, seaworthy boat to get five miles down the coast in ten minutes. But he'd looked at the sign at the marina, and those babies rented for 140 dollars per hour. Lee glanced out across the water as a moderate breeze ruffled his hair. It was early afternoon, and the trades were picking up. The choppy water would slow them down even more.

He could call Peterson in a few minutes and tell him about the yacht, even if they hadn't verified that it was the trafficker's vessel, but if that drew Peterson away from another important lead, Lee might regret his decision for the rest of his life. No. They needed to do this part of the investigation on their own.

Grandfather parked. He motioned for Lee to follow, then he and Katie ran towards the boats in the marina. By the time Lee caught up with them, a short Asian man was handing keys to Granddad. The man pointed towards a small catamaran with two large outboard engines on the back. The boat looked tailor-made for their purposes.

Five minutes later, Granddad had maneuvered the boat out of the marina, and they were skimming the choppy aqua-blue water at better than forty miles per hour.

They still had four or five miles to go. "Can this thing go any faster?"

Granddad responded with his lead foot.

The boat surged ahead, throwing Lee into the back of the boat. Spray flew all around them cooling the heat from the sun while creating small rainbows that appeared and disappeared at the whims of the mist and the angle of the sun.

At this speed, they would be nearing Turtle Town in less than five minutes. Lee glanced at Katie, unbuttoning her blouse. It flew into the back of the boat and she unzipped her shorts. "Katie, what do you think you're doing?"

"Don't worry. This is my swimsuit underneath. Oh yes...when Granddad talked to him on the phone, his cousin said the snorkeling gear is in the bin under your seat."

So Granddad had thought this through already. They could pretend to be snorkeling Turtle Town and get close to the yacht without tipping their hand. He looked at Granddad, smiled, and gave him thumbs up.

Granddad responded with a heavier lead foot.

The choppiness of the water had decreased over the past mile. He scanned the sea around them then looked up at the mountain. They were entering the lee of Haleakala, an area where today the trade winds were impeded by the big mountain. Good. They'd be able to see more while they were in the water than if the swells were larger.

"Where's your swimsuit, Lee?"

He glanced up at Katie and his breath caught in his throat. Standing there in her two-piece swimsuit, long, blonde hair flying in the breeze, she was a stunning beauty. She would bring a continuous stream of guys to their house. His smart, courageous future daughter was as beautiful as her future mother. Jennifer and he would have their hands full—

Jennifer.

Everything was predicated on saving her. Otherwise, he could lose Katie, too.

Granddad slowed as they approached an area of boats and swimmers.

Lee put his wallet in a small compartment by the wheel, then pulled off his shirt, shoes, and socks. He grabbed two pairs of fins and a couple of masks with snorkels from the bin. "Katie, how strong of a swimmer are you?"

She took the equipment and smiled. "Very. But I've never used one of these things." She held up the snorkel.

He positioned the mask and snorkel on her head, and gave her a couple of pointers. When he glanced up, Granddad cut the engine back to an idle.

"Is that the yacht?" Granddad nodded his head in the direction of a large, blue vessel, as Lee pulled his cell phone from his shorts pocket.

"That's it. Here's my cell, Granddad. If any other boat approaches the yacht while Katie and I are in the water, hit number five on my speed dial, like this. Peterson will answer. Just tell him—"

"I know what to tell him, Lee." Granddad slid the

cell phone in beside Lee's wallet. "Now you and Katie go pretend to chase turtles. And be careful. Don't get too close. We can't make them feel threatened or they might threaten us."

"Did you hear Granddad, Katie?"

"I heard. I'll pretend to be looking for turtles, and as I roll around in the water, I can catch glimpses of the yacht to—"

"To identify the people on board. Get good descriptions of them. If Peterson has suspicions about the ringleader, our description could confirm them, bringing the Coast Guard, the MPD, and the FBI down on these guys in a matter of minutes."

"Granddad, if we give you the signal"—Lee raised his closed fist and shook it—"you call Peterson immediately and declare an emergency, got it?"

Grandfather nodded.

"OK. Into the water, Katie."

They both jumped over the side and soon were bobbing in the water.

Katie pulled the snorkel from her mouth." It's warm, Lee. Like bathwater."

"That's why people pay thousands of dollars to come here. Now, look around for turtles and...other things, but don't get too far away from me."

Katie's snorkel went back into her mouth, and she headed to the seaward side of the big yacht's bow.

Lee followed her.

In a few seconds, a large turtle surfaced directly in front of Katie. Her head came up for an above-the-water look, and then went back down. She swam hard to catch the fascinating sea creature.

Movement across the water drew Lee's gaze. A big catamaran was heading straight for the yacht. The man standing on the bow was of Middle Eastern descent, and his gaze was locked on the blue yacht. The catamaran slowed and inched towards the yacht. Was this the trafficker's customer?

23

Franklin James stood on the bow of his yacht watching the white catamaran approach. This transfer would come off as planned, or James would immediately distance himself from the whole mess. A one-hundred-pound weight on her ankle restraint and a quick drop into one thousand feet of water would be ample distance.

When the prince's catamaran moved within fifty yards of his yacht, James began barking orders. "Snake, get the assault rifle. Keep the gun out of sight of anyone who may be watching."

Mack's stocky form approached James from behind Snake. "Mack, you get the merchandise ready. On my signal, she goes out the door, over the side, and down onto the deck of the other boat. Understood?"

"Understood, boss."

"Until the transfer, wait outside the cabin door. Watch for any signs of trouble. I'll give you the signal to get her after the catamaran draws near. Then you will complete the transfer as quickly as possible."

"Got it." Mack walked down the port side of the yacht and resumed his guard post by the cabin door.

Snake appeared in a few seconds standing forward, slightly to the port side, with the weapon clamped tightly to his leg.

James smiled. From one hundred yards away, the gun would not be visible to anyone.

Snake gestured towards something on the starboard side.

When James glanced that direction, he saw a snorkeler too close for his comfort. Since all the action would be on the port side, if they hurried, they could still pull this off.

He waited a few more seconds. The prince's boat was only twenty-five yards away and moving slowly towards the yacht. When James gave his signal, Mack turned and reached for the cabin door.

****

Jennifer's fierce blow cracked the ashtray in half. Half she held, the other half bounced across the floor and slid under the edge of the bed.

She glanced up at the guard's silhouette. It was gone. There were voices coming from somewhere outside. A deep rumble came from something near. Was another boat approaching? The sound sent her heart pounding and adrenaline coursing through her bloodstream.

She sat down on the floor outside the bathroom door, wedged the broken half of the ashtray between her feet, and began sawing on her wrist restraints.

The sharp edge of the ashtray cut through the wrist restraints far enough for her to break them. It'd taken less than a minute of sawing. She quickly grabbed the shard of ashtray in her hands and sawed furiously on the ankle restraints.

Footsteps sounded outside the door. The guard's silhouette moved on the sunlit curtain. The door handle turned.

Jennifer made one more violent slice with the

ashtray and her ankles broke free.

The door swung open. Mack stepped into the room from the bright sunlight outside.

Realizing it would take a moment for his eyes to adjust, Jennifer jumped up, the ashtray in hand, and leaped towards him.

Mack tried to back away from the body hurtling at him.

Jennifer's vicious kick powered by her emotions, adrenaline, and her consuming desire to reach Lee's arms again, smashed into Mack's face. The kick drove his head backward, where it cracked hard on the wall.

She delivered her second kick to a vulnerable spot below Mack's belt. He grunted and slumped forward.

Jennifer drove the ashtray shard deep into the side of Mack's neck. His loud howl would surely bring help.

When blood spurted from the wound on Mack's neck, he frantically ripped at the bedding, seeking something to pack over his wound. A single glance at Mack told her his role in the fight was over.

She leapt out the door towards the railing. There was movement to her left. And…what was this? A boat had pulled alongside the yacht and the space between the two vessels had nearly closed.

Jennifer dove over the railing, praying she wouldn't be crushed between the two vessels.

As she flew over the rail, she saw Snake in her peripheral vision. He was raising an assault rifle.

The staccato burping of an automatic weapon sounded when Jennifer's back bounced off the approaching catamaran. After the hard bump, she slid into the water.

The warm saltwater amplified the sting of the

abrasion on her back. She pulled hard for the bottom and tried to ignore the pain. Bubbly lines traced the path of bullets in the water beside her. She needed to go deeper.

Had she taken a deep enough breath? It didn't matter. The impact on her back had knocked most of it out of her.

With her breath mostly gone, she couldn't swim far under water. How could she avoid the bullets? By swimming under the catamaran and coming up on the far side? Could she make it even that short distance?

Her lungs already burned with oxygen deprivation. The adrenaline only magnified her oxygen craving.

Kicking hard, she saw light at the far side of the catamaran's hull.

Catamaran. What was she thinking? Jennifer pulled for the surface between the two sides of the catamaran. She drew a deep breath when her head broke water at about midship. She looked around her. Light blinded her from the front of the vessel. If someone leaned over the bow, they could peer between the two hulls. They would spot her. She prayed that wouldn't happen for a few more seconds.

Jennifer took four deep breaths and pushed her body under. She continued downward until she was about ten feet under, probably deep enough to be safe from the assault rifle's bullets. Using the orientation of the catamaran to determine her direction, she estimated the direction of the large resort hotel and swam under water towards it.

The next time she came up for air, the gunman may have moved to the catamaran where he could fire at her. She would stay down until she started to black out. Jennifer purposely lost herself in prayer to counter the message her lungs were screaming and to fight the urge to swim to the surface.

Lord, help me now...to keep going...to reach the shore...to reach Lee.

She repeated the prayer until her vision became fuzzy, until the oxygen-starved muscles in her legs refused to kick, until her body became still in the water.

24

James's door of opportunity had shut. Almost single-handedly, a 110-pound woman with an IQ double her weight had slammed the door shut and made him out to be a fool.

Goals change. James's goal was now to prevent a prison door from slamming shut with him inside. He snagged Snake's binoculars with one hand and ran to the bow of the yacht. As the catamaran and his yacht moved apart, his yacht had cut off the snorkeler from his boat.

The snorkeler pushed his mask up onto his forehead and appeared to be surveying the situation.

James trained the binoculars on the snorkeler. Reality struck him like a bolt of lightning.

The blonde-haired princess. But how?

Realization of his situation sent another lightning bolt through James's rigid body. Too many people knew his location. With the island-wide law-enforcement presence, escaping with his life became his number one priority.

"Snake."

The slender man with the assault rifle stopped scanning the water for Jennifer Akihara-Brandt and turned towards him. "What, Mr. James?"

"Forget her. Get in the water and bring *her* on board." He pointed to the girl a few feet from the yacht's bow.

Snake shook his head and frowned. "You sure about this?"

"Do it now, Snake. We might need a hostage."

Snake's eyes widened as he stared at his boss for a moment.

So Snake understood the extent of the danger now. Good. Perhaps it would motivate him.

Snake grabbed the spear gun from the storage cabinet beside him. He slipped off his sandals, ran to the bow of the yacht, and jumped over the railing.

James only hope of keeping his identity and location concealed long enough to escape was to kill the two men in the boat, capture the blonde in the water, and hope they had fatally wounded Jennifer Akihara-Brandt. Or hope the Iranians got her if she somehow made it to shore. He felt certain the pesky Iranians were watching. Without even knowing it, the Iranians had become his rear guard.

His Gulfstream was fueled and ready to fly at Kahului airport. But first, he had to get there, and he would sacrifice anyone and anything but himself and his pilot to reach his plane.

The sound of whining outboard engines grew louder.

James took the gun and crossed the deck towards the noise. The men in the boat were trying to circle his yacht to the side where Snake and the girl were. He couldn't allow that.

He started to call to Mack for help, but saw him lying on his side coughing and choking while holding a bloodstained wad of fabric to his neck. He could forget about Mack.

James waited for a good shot. When the boat rounded the bow, fifty yards out, he fired a burst.

The boat veered out of control when both men dropped to the deck. But they got up and made another run, getting further around the yacht before his gunfire drove them away.

Now the boat raced away from him headed due south, still on the side where Snake and the girl were swimming in the water. He fired again, but the boat was out of range.

They would call the authorities. Within the hour these waters would be teeming with Coast Guard personnel, Maui policemen, FBI agents, and who knows what else?

James's mind moved ahead with his plan, a plan that would free him from the clutches of the law, a plan that would get him back to Southeast Asia, a plan that relied on using the blonde-haired princess as his hostage.

****

Katie had blown it. She felt like a foolish schoolgirl. She *was* a foolish schoolgirl and it may cost her life.

Why did I follow the turtle so far? What was I thinking?

Everything seemed to have changed in an instant. But what really happened?

First, the yacht had moved. Then there was gunfire.

Thoughts of what the gunfire might mean tied her stomach into one big knot. If it cramped any harder, here in the water, she could be in serious trouble.

A movement near the bow of the yacht caught her attention. Someone had jumped overboard. She *was* in trouble, but it had nothing to do with cramps.

Katie gasped as a man's head burst out of the water less than six feet from her. He thrust one end of a long object at her. She gasped again when she recognized the menacing spearhead loaded in the spear gun that was pointed at her face.

"Come with me...unless you're into body piercing."

The man's voice was all air, like a hiss, like a snake. She was too stunned and frightened to move.

"Where shall we do the first piercing? Nose or belly button?" the man hissed.

She needed to think, to collect her wits, but they were scattered to the four corners of—

"OK, let's do the nose." He aimed the spear gun at her face.

"No! I'm coming." Katie fluttered her fins and moved a couple of feet closer to the man.

"Smart girl. Cute, too. No...more like a blonde-haired, blue-eyed princess."

That's what the traffickers who captured her near Seattle had called her. Coincidence? Katie doubted that.

"Swim around me, towards the boat. Do it now!"

She complied. *Lee, I'm sorry. So sorry. I didn't think.*

"Swim towards the ladder. You will go up it first. Leave your gear in the water. You won't need it."

Katie's gaze followed the ladder to the top. Silhouetted against the blue sky, was the form of a tall man holding an assault rifle.

The man with the rifle whirled and ran for the far side of the boat.

A boat motor revved up. The rifle fired...in automatic mode.

A second burst of fire sounded, nearly drowned out by the roar of boat engines. It sounded like Granddad's boat.

Please keep them safe.

A third burst of gunfire. The boat sounded farther away. A booming voice spewed a garbage can full of gutter language and some other words Katie had never heard, but they didn't sound good. She took the man's response as a good sign.

But did the droning boat motors mean Granddad and Lee got away without being hit? Her hand grabbed the ladder attached to the side of the blue yacht, and she froze.

"Off with the snorkeling gear," the man with the spear gun hissed at her.

Katie willed her frozen muscles to move. She pulled off her mask and snorkel. They floated on the water. She slipped out of her fins and watched them sink slowly into the depths of the blue water. Is that where she would end up when they were through with her?

A sharp sting radiated from a spot on her back. He had shoved the spear gun against her skin.

"Up the ladder, princess."

Was it better to have it out right here than to endure whatever waited for her on the yacht?

Pain. The spear cut through her skin, followed by the tickling sensation of blood trickling down her back.

"Move! Now!"

I've got no choice.

Slowly Katie climbed the ladder towards the man with the gun and an ominous, and possibly very short, future.

25

A disturbance on board the yacht drew Lee's attention. He froze in the water when an automatic rifle went off like a string of firecrackers. The catamaran and the yacht swung apart. Now the action was all on the opposite side of the yacht.

Lee glanced back towards Katie and the big turtle she had followed. Katie was gone, cut off from his sight by the moving bow of the yacht. She was on the wrong side of the yacht and possibly in serious danger.

"Katie, come back!"

No use yelling right now. The roar of the engines from the two boats maneuvering in the water drowned out his voice.

A gunman and another man appeared on the bow of the yacht. The gunman pointed towards the water. Towards Katie.

Now he was certain she was in danger.

Lee whirled in the water to swim back to Granddad for help, but stopped when someone jumped from the yacht into the water. The man held something in one hand, something very long, something that looked like a spear gun. He prayed it wasn't.

With a sudden surge of adrenaline and his fins fluttering, Lee propelled his body through the water at an incredible speed.

Granddad swung the boat alongside, and Lee

pulled himself onto it.

"They cut Katie off and someone on the yacht jumped in to get her. I think he had a spear gun."

At Lee's words, Granddad cranked the wheel and hit the throttle. Powerful engines tilted the boat sharply as they spun a one-eighty and headed around the bow of the yacht.

"Careful, Granddad. They've got automatic weapons. They already fired at something in—"

Lee stopped in mid sentence. The shots were fired towards the rear of the yacht. They hadn't fired at Katie. She was near the bow.

Jennifer!

Had she tried to escape? Was the catamaran the customer's boat? The one who was trying to buy Jennifer? If she waited this long, it must have been an attempt born of desperation more than opportunity.

A thought hit him out of the blue. Jennifer or Katie? What if he could only save one of them? Could he make a choice? Would a good God require him to do that?

A staccato burping noise jolted Lee out of his musings. Water exploded upward in a dotted line of splashes. The dotted line headed straight for the boat. Straight for Granddad.

Lee hooked Granddad with an arm. He yanked the small man all the way to the back of the boat. The line of bullets bisected the boat. The burst of gunfire ended.

Granddad's last hand to leave the wheel had jerked it to the left. Without a pilot, the boat turned towards the bow of the yacht. The throttle was three-quarters open.

Lee dove for the wheel and another line the bullets

cut a swath through the spot his body had vacated. It narrowly missed Granddad.

Lee yanked the wheel to the right. The boat veered away from the yacht.

Granddad crawled over a seat, stood beside Lee and opened the throttle...all the way. The powerful boat surged forward, knocking Lee off his feet. It rose onto a plane and flew across the flat water at sixty miles per hour, headed due south, away from the yacht, away from the bullets, and away from Katie.

Lee grabbed his cell phone from the compartment by the wheel where Granddad had placed it.

Granddad slid behind the wheel and took full control of the boat. He left the throttle wide open.

There were no more shots. At least none that Lee heard. But concern for Jennifer and now Katie assaulted him with a mind-chilling fear, a brain freeze with an emotional source.

He tried to think, but the icy fear had paralyzed his mind.

"Granddad?" He managed to shove the word out of his mouth.

Granddad backed off on the throttle. "Yes, Lee."

They fired the first shots down into the water, between the yacht and the catamaran. I think that—"

"That we should pray for Jennifer." Granddad interjected.

"Yeah. Maybe that was her only chance to try to escape before..." He couldn't finish the sentence.

"I think you're right, Lee. That sounds like my granddaughter. She has a mental toughness that accomplishes amazing things. But we need to pray she made it and that she is unharmed."

Lee nodded as a tight knot in his gut turned to

nausea. He choked off the urge to vomit and looked at the cell phone in his trembling hand. "I should call Peterson now."

Granddad sighed heavily. "Yes." The man seldom frowned, but twin frown lines invaded his stoic brow. "You need to call Peterson."

Granddad turned the boat around and headed north between the yacht and the shoreline. He maintained a course that would keep them out of firing range when they passed the yacht.

Lee flipped his cell open. He sought words to describe to the FBI agent all that had transpired in those few furious seconds.

When he had collected enough words, Lee slid his finger over the speed dial button of his cell. His phone rang, giving him a jolt that nearly made him drop it. Who would be calling? Peterson? Ramirez? He glanced at the caller ID. It was a local number, but one he didn't recognize.

26

Jennifer, you can't let them shoot you. You've come too far.

The words came from the muddle of thoughts running through the circuits of her oxygen-starved brain.

Her legs dangled in the water, without the strength to move. Her body floated upward, face down, the dead man's float. Barely aware that she would soon surface, Jennifer managed to rotate her body into a face-up position.

Her face broke the surface and felt the warm sun as she sucked hard, filling her lungs with that marvelous mixture of gases that sustained life on the planet. She expelled the first batch of air and filled her lungs again. Her head began to clear, and she took greater care to allow only her face to show above the water.

She dared not raise her head to look around, but she had to be sure of where she was. After she turned her body several degrees, a large white resort became clearly visible. The sprawling structure was situated on a small hill above the beach. Jennifer swiveled, aligning her feet with the resort, took a deep breath, and pushed her body under with her hands.

She wouldn't have to swim as deep now. The choppy water and the fact that surfacing drew no more shots meant she could swim only three feet under the surface where there was less pressure on her chest and the water was warmer.

The resort wasn't her real destination. She was swimming to Lee. At that thought a tremendous surge of adrenaline shot through her body. She swam furiously in the direction of resort.

In another thirty seconds, she surfaced and drew a few breaths, then submerged and swam hard for the shore.

Lee was waiting. Probably wondering if she was dead, or worse. She needed to feel his arms around her, to tell him she hadn't been harmed, to listen to his heartbeat, and press her lips against his. There was more, a lot more waiting. Their wedding night had been interrupted by cruel men with cruel intentions. But they were behind her now. They were in the past and Lee was her future. She took another breath and started a one-hundred-yard swimming sprint to the shore.

A small, partially hidden cove lay to her right. Jennifer swam towards it, careful to avoid the volcanic rocks protruding out of the water only slightly farther to her right. A gentle wave caught her body. She relaxed and rode it into the cove until her knees drug in the gritty, golden sand.

When Jennifer stood, she was hidden to all boats except those directly seaward from the narrow cove. She scanned the narrow section of water. No boats.

She waded into the cove and spotted a small path leading up to the main beach trail. She took it.

On the beach trail there were many people walking, talking, oblivious to her ordeal. That she was standing here, having faced death moments before, was surreal. Perhaps she needed to pinch herself to be convinced of this reality. No. What she needed was a phone.

Jennifer looked to her left, towards the Grand Wailea Resort. Surely there would be phones there. Or she could run down onto the beach and ask to borrow someone's cell phone.

She glanced to her right. Not twenty-five yards down the trail was a large concession stand, something like a small convenience store. As she jogged towards it, she felt a strand of nylon whipping her ankle and another slapping against her wrist. She had neither the means nor the will to remove them now, only a desperate drive to hear Lee's voice.

Jennifer sought appropriate words to explain her situation as she slowed near the stand. A young man stood by a cash register and a young woman was making an espresso drink. She chose the man. "Please, I need to use your phone. I'm the girl from the Amber Alert. I escaped and—"

"How did you...? Never mind. Here's my cell. Are you OK?"

She took the phone. "Yes. But I would be more OK if you have something to cut these restraints off." She shook the tie dangling from her wrist.

He reached into his pocket, pulled out a knife, then opened and locked the blade. "Be careful, it's really sharp."

She took it, cut the ties from her feet and hands, and then slammed them into a trash can like an NBA player at the end of a fast break. "Thanks." She handed the man his knife and dialed Lee's cell number.

"Please answer, Lee. Please answer," she whispered after two rings.

After the third ring, she heard his voice. Tears

filled her eyes. Jennifer opened her mouth, but emotions stopped her voice.

"Hello. Who is this?"

"It's Jennifer. I escaped."

"Jennifer…" A sharp blast of air created a staticky sound. After another heavy breath, Lee's voice returned. "I heard the shots." Now his voice sounded tense, almost frantic." Did they hit you? Are you OK?"

Shots? Hit me? What was he—how did he know? "Lee, where are you?"

"Jenn!" he shouted in frustration. "Are you OK?"

"Yes, I'm OK. But where are you?"

"I'm in a boat with Granddad. We're near Wailea."

"Granddad? I don't understand, Lee. What are—"

"Jenn, you need to tell me where you are."

"I'm on the beach trail near the Grand Wailea Resort, at a concession stand. Please come and get me."

"We're not far away. I'm coming, and I'll only be two or three minutes. But listen, there are some Iranian agents looking for you. Two of them were on that beach trail about a quarter mile south of you a few minutes ago. They look Middle Eastern. One is tall, the other short and stocky and they're—"

"What colors are they wearing?"

"Red or maroon and white, I think."

She looked southward down the trail and gasped. "I see them. They're coming towards me. About fifty yards away."

"Run, Jenn. Try security in the resort lobby. Or hide with the woman in Chapel Wing room 414. That's Chapel Wing room 414. I'm coming, and I'll call Peterson on the way."

Peterson?

"I love you, Lee." She shoved the phone at its

owner. "Those two men are after me." She pointed to the men now running towards her. "Please call 911."

She sprinted north on the trail towards the resort, the salt water on her skin, dried by the sun, cracking with each stride. After dodging an elderly couple, Jennifer glanced back at the stand. The two men sprinted towards her, less than fifty yards away.

She still wore her wet sandals. Her feet slipped badly in them, nearly causing her to fall. She jumped onto the grass, ripped off her sandals, and glanced back. The two men had closed to within thirty yards.

Jennifer veered off the trail across the grassy grounds of the resort. She scanned the area, looking for a place to lose the two men and then cut back to her left, sprinted by the chapel. No place to hide there.

She turned up the hill towards the resort. The main entrance lay to her right.

The men had split up. One cut off her path to the main entrance, the other dogged her.

Like a wolf pack, the two ran her down, cutting off her access to any place of help, to any place to hide.

She spotted a smaller resort entrance straight up the hill from the chapel. Inside the resort she would fine hallways, banquet rooms, elevators, stairwells, places she could elude them even if she couldn't get to the hotel security people.

Jennifer clenched her jaw and began an all-out sprint across the grass straight towards the entrance. A sign ahead said Chapel Wing Entrance. The room Lee mentioned was on the Chapel Wing. Room number 414. She couldn't imagine what significance the room had, and she couldn't enter a guest's room with two men close behind her.

She would have to use the resort as a maze to lose

them. Only thirty yards to the doorway, but the man dogging her trailed by less than twenty yards. Still no sirens.

Had the cashier called 911? Please, Lee. Hurry.

27

While Katie climbed the ladder towards the deck of the yacht, the man with the reptilian voice prodded her with the spear. He obviously enjoyed doing that. She sensed a deep-seated cruelty in him that she would be careful to avoid inciting.

What did these men want with her? Had they captured her simply because she got too close? And where was Jenn?

Katie determined to keep her eyes and ears open, gather all of the information she could, and try to formulate a plan of escape. But first, she had to find Jenn. Together, they could take out one of the men and get away.

After two more painful prods with the spear, Katie reached the top of the ladder. The tall man with the rifle grabbed her arm with his other hand and yanked her onto the deck.

She was five feet nine and weighed nearly 130 pounds, but the man handled her weight as if she were a bag of groceries.

"Look at me!" The tall man's voice and posture said he was used to giving commands and having people obey him.

She looked up into a darkly tanned face that exuded evil. His eyes were cold, lifeless. Katie shuddered. She'd been told about demonic influence. This man fit the description she had formed in her mind. She would cower, pretend to be helpless, and maybe she would get a chance to use the karate Granddad had taught her. Maybe she would find some other way of escape. She looked into the man's evil face again and shuddered. Maybe she should just trust the God who was always with her to take care of the details.

"Do as you're told, princess, or the sharks will have a feast. Do you understand?" He cupped her chin and lifted her head.

She nodded, but avoided his eyes. She didn't want to see them. Didn't want them seeing her intentions, seeing that she wanted to deliver a brutal kick right between those dead eyes and dive into the water.

When she had reached her limit for enduring this man's scrutiny, he pulled his gaze from her.

Though the sun was warm, the cooling of the trades blowing across her wet skin and the coldness of the man's eyes chilled Katie to the bone.

"Snake, put her in the guest bedroom and be sure to remove the little weapon the previous guest left behind."

They were talking about Jennifer. Katie lowered her head and listened. So Snake was the hissing man's name. These people seemed to get everything in life wrong. But they had gotten something right. The man *was* a snake.

"Did you see any signs of her while I was in the water?" Snake asked.

Did that mean Jenn had escaped?

"No signs. No blood in the water. Nothing," the head guy said.

Snake shook his head. "That could mean big trouble for—"

"I'm fully aware of that. Now get this girl inside the cabin, out of sight."

Snake took her arm, jammed the spear in her back, and pushed her towards the port side of the yacht.

"How's Mack doing?" Snake asked as he pushed her along.

"Not good. Our million-dollar baby nearly severed his jugular. He's stretched out on a bed, bleeding. Not sure if he's going to make it."

Snake jerked her to a stop and turned towards the tall man. "Sounds like Mack's not going to be much help. That only leaves you, me, and the captain."

"But we have a hostage if we need one."

"If?" Snake laughed in a staccato of hisses. "We'll need her before this day's over." He prodded her ahead with the spear.

So that's what she was to them, a hostage. Jenn *had* escaped, nearly killing one of the men in the process. Katie prayed Jenn was safe, and she prayed for a chance to do what her future mother had done.

Her loathing of these men mushroomed out of control. She wanted to replicate in great detail what Jenn must have done to them. She would eventually beg for God's forgiveness, but right now, cutting Snake's throat and cutting off his hissing voice in the process would give her great satisfaction.

Snake jerked her to a stop. "Open the door."

Katie twisted the handle and pushed open the door. A siren sounded in the distance. Then several more. The wop, wop, wop, of a helicopter's rotor grew louder. Snake shoved her inside, and then shoved her to the floor.

She was in a bedroom. The carpet reeked of cigarette smoke. She pulled her head up from the foul-smelling carpet and sneezed.

"Not you too?"

"I can't breathe in here. I'm allergic to cig—"

"Then don't breathe." Snake's hissing chuckle sounded like someone wheezing. "If you don't shut up, I'll end your breathing problem right now." He shoved her head down onto the carpet.

Snake pulled several nylon ties from his pocket and prodded her with his spear. "Don't move except to breathe...if you can." He chuckled and stepped to the bed, where he picked up a roll of duct tape.

Katie stared at the roll of tape, picturing tape covering her mouth. An uncontrollable terror nearly took her sanity. When he peeled off a length of tape, Katie's terror exploded into a panic attack. When he approached her with the tape, she rolled, kicked, wiggled, anything to get away.

He dealt her a savage blow, a backhand across her face, and jammed the spear hard against her throat.

"Stop! Now! Or I'll pull the trigger."

Katie froze. Rationality returned, but her heart still threatened to burst from the pressure of her pulse.

He pulled the spear head back a couple of inches from her neck. "Turn over on your stomach."

She had to tell him. He couldn't tape her mouth, or....

"Turn over now."

She winced as the sharp spearhead broke the skin on her neck. Blood trickled down her neck. Slowly Katie rolled over.

He placed her ankles on the floor straddling the corner bed post, and pulled two sets of restraints around her ankles, tying her to the bed.

She sat up on the floor. "If you tape my mouth, I'll

smother. I'm allergic to cigarette smoke."

The restraints cut into her wrists as Snake pulled them tight behind her back.

"Please. You've got to believe me. I promise to be quiet if—"

"Oh, you'll be quiet all right."

He wrenched her head to one side and slapped a length to the tape over her mouth.

Before he could smooth the tape, Katie's fear exploded into sheer terror.

Snake laughed his wheezy laugh as she writhed on the floor.

One thought screamed inside her head in an endless loop, "I can't breathe!"

She screamed it from her mouth, but the tape forced it back down her throat, choking her, making, her cough, inciting another choking spasm.

Was it a few minutes or an eternity later? She didn't know and couldn't tell. But she lay exhausted on the smoky carpet, drenched in sweat and breathing through her nose. Maybe she *could* do this. Maybe she *could* suppress the panic. She'd heard that adrenaline acted like an antihistamine. But having repeated panic attacks to stay alive didn't seem much better than the alternative.

Snake sat in a chair watching her with a smirk on his face. He enjoyed people's suffering. If she could, Katie would've planted a foot stomp squarely on those smirking lips.

Her anger grew until it masked her panic. Yes, she could do this. She *would* do this.

Snake stood and stepped to the door. He stooped and picked up an object on the floor, lying against the wall. "Our million-dollar baby nearly cut Mack's head

off with this ash tray. The other half is in the water."
He walked around the room and returned to where
Katie lay. "Safe enough for even a toddler like you.
Enjoy your stay, princess."

Snake grabbed his spear gun and left Katie alone
to wage war with her wheezing and her worry about
the panic attack that felt only seconds away.

28

Lee closed his cell, realizing he hadn't told Jennifer about Katie. Maybe that was best for now. She didn't need any distractions. He whirled towards Jennifer's grandfather. "Granddad, Jennifer's running along the beach trail to the Grand Wailea with two Iranians in pursuit."

"Is she OK?"

"Right now she is, but I need to get there ASAP. How fast can you get me to the beach behind the resort? And I need my cell. It's supposed to be water-resistant. It can take a dunk, but I wouldn't want to go for a swim with it. We need to get in close."

Granddad smiled. "I can get you into shallow water so you don't have to swim."

"But you might run this thing aground."

"Not to worry, Lee. I can do this. It's called the slingshot maneuver."

I hope he's not serious. "Granddad, isn't that something police do using a patrol car on pavement after they've practiced it?"

"Car, boat, pavement, water…it works the same. You'll see."

"But what if you get in too close and run the boat—"

"Don't worry, Lee. Water is much softer than pavement. Trust me." He opened the throttle.

Lee retrieved his wallet from where he had placed

it, slipped out Ramirez's card, and jotted Peterson's cell number on the back. "You call Peterson and tell him about Katie. This could end up being a hostage situation. We'll need the FBI to rescue her. I'll check with you once Jennifer is safe. If for any reason I can't reach you, then I'll call Peterson."

"After I call Peterson, I'll watch the yacht from a safe distance. If they move Katie, we need to know about it." Granddad shot him a glance.

"Sounds like a plan."

The boat skimmed the water at sixty miles per hour, headed directly for Wailea Beach.

"Are you sure about this slingshot—"

"Like I said, trust me, Lee. It will work."

"Trust me, he says. When do I have to trust you?"

"In about fifteen or twenty seconds. Stand on the seat, hold your cell phone over your head, and get ready to jump towards shore."

Lee quickly surveyed the inlet. The snorkelers were all along the volcanic rocks at either end of the beach. He focused on Wailea Beach. It rushed at them at an insane rate. *How can Granddad stop in—*

Lee went airborne, pushing off his toes at the last second as the boat spun ninety degrees and nearly stopped in the water. The maneuver launched Lee off-balance. He flew in a flat arc towards shore. With his arms flailing and legs churning like a long jumper, he struggled to regain his balance and enter the water feet first.

Fifty feet closer to shore, Lee butt-flopped with a pop in three feet of water. His cell may have briefly gone under. His rear stung from the slap the water gave it, but he had survived Granddad's slingshot. He opened his phone. Its display indicated his cell had also survived.

Shaking his head then wiping saltwater from his eyes, Lee stood and gave Granddad a thumbs up. Then he ran a hand over his backside to make sure his cargo shorts weren't split.

When Granddad waved him towards the resort, every sunbather on the beach stood, staring at the spectacle.

The spectacle scampered out of the water and broke into an all-out sprint towards what looked like the main entrance on the beach side of the hotel. Lee prayed he would find Jennifer safe inside.

Knowing that she was inside the door sent his heart and lungs into overdrive. He sprinted the 150 yards across the grass to the door, sending clods of turf flying from his shoes like a racehorse.

He dodged a waiter exiting the door and dodged two more as he ran through a large dining room. Lee sprinted down a long corridor towards the main desk. He rounded a corner and jerked to a stop when the counter hit him in the stomach. His upper body flew across the counter, and his protruding face stared into the wide eyes of the short clerk, barely a foot in front of him.

"Can...Can I help—"

"Call the police. Two terrorists are chasing my wife, the woman in the Amber Alert."

"Terrorists? Police? Amber Alert? Are you sure?"

He didn't have time for this. "Just do it, you knucklehead! Now, has anyone seen them?"

The young man appeared to recover from his initial shock. "There's some kind of disturbance that security is monitoring on the—"

"Where is it? Lee yelled, pounding the counter

with his fist.

The clerk backed away from him, his gaze darting from Lee's face to his fist. The young man pointed to a corridor on the north side of the building. "It's...it's on the first floor, Chapel wing...people are running and they're—"

Lee charged for the Chapel Wing. As he approached the entrance to the wing he slowed.

The sounds of running feet echoed in the Chapel Overlook concourse.

Jennifer sprinted out of the concourse but turned away from Lee towards the dining room. She ran barefoot, hardly making a sound. The clomping of shoes grew louder.

Lee ran to the wing thirty yards away.

A short, stocky man flew out and turned the direction Jennifer had run.

He had missed the short man, so Lee accelerated as he heard a second man coming. When a lanky man emerged, Lee hit him as hard as he could, just like he had been taught by his high school football coach, head in front, shoulder driving through the hips, arms clamping like two-by-fours, legs running like the person is still ten feet away when you make contact.

Lights flashed at the incredible impact. The running man's thigh dealt Lee's cheek a stunning blow. But the force of the tackle whipped the man's head over Lee. The backlash sent the guy's head flying the opposite direction into a stone wall.

Despite the lightning flash and his ringing ears, Lee heard the man's head hit the wall, sounding like a softball slugged for an extra-base hit.

When Lee stood, he shook his head to knock the cobwebs loose. Then he waited for the dazed, detached feeling to be replaced by reality. In what seemed like only a few seconds, Lee was back.

He looked at the man on the floor. One side of the man's face was covered in blood oozing from a gaping split in his scalp. He was out cold, not moving. He didn't appear to be breathing, and Lee wasn't going to stop to help him.

Lee took off in the direction Jennifer had disappeared, towards the big dining room.

When he turned the corner to enter, the short stocky Iranian flew by him. He had reversed direction. He was running the opposite direction as Jennifer and obviously planned to intercept her on the other side of the big loop forming the first floor of the resort.

Lee hesitated, then turned to run after the stocky man, but Jennifer emerged from the dining room. She had reversed direction, too.

Smart girl.

He hooked Jennifer with an arm and pulled her to his right, towards the Chapel wing elevator door, and pressed the button. "Fourth floor, Jenn, 414, Bertha Renner. Love you. See you there."

"But, Lee—"

He pushed her inside and ran opposite the direction the Iranian had run.

Sirens wailed in the distance. As Lee ran through the dining room, they grew louder. Would the man give up the chase now? The guy must have seen his friend out on the floor covered in blood. No. Even that didn't stop the man.

Lee stepped into the dining room, lined up with the far corner, giving him a straight shot at it, and waited for the sound of running feet.

He heard shots from two different guns. This

added an extra measure of uncertainty to what he was doing. The Iranian could take him out with a single shot unless…

Lee moved to within ten yards of the corner, positioned his feet to run, waited, and listened. The sound of running feet grew louder. He tried to picture where the man was by the sounds, tried to time his run to hit the guy at the corner, tried to picture the man's body slamming into the floor like a helpless quarterback being blindsided.

Here he comes.

Lee broke from his starting posture and streaked towards the corner. He arrived in tackling position just as a shoe hit the floor. Lee executed a picture perfect tackle. His shoulder struck the man's thighs and took him down hard.

The impact from a knee sent another flash of light through Lee's head. He crashed onto the floor on top of the man. Lee raised his fist to smash whatever first appeared smashable. When the two stopped sliding, Lee stopped his fist. He was staring into the face of Officer Yagi.

"Brandt don't hit me, or I'll have you arrested." Yagi groaned as he rolled and pushed up onto his knees. "Why did you tackle me anyway?"

"Where's the short Iranian dude? He was running this way. I was planning to take him out."

Yagi pushed up into a kneeling position, shook his head a few times, and then rose to his feet. "The Iranian dude got himself shot. He pulled a gun on us when we came in. Kaai had to shoot him."

"Then what were you doing running towards the restaurant?"

Yagi shook his head again. "Man, where'd you

learn to tackle like that?"

Lee stood and rubbed his jaw. "Where'd you get legs like that? Your knee nearly knocked me out. But you didn't answer my question."

"What question?"

"Come on. I didn't hit you *that* hard. Why were you running around this corner?"

"They told me there was another Iranian down here. A tall dude, bleeding all over the floor."

Lee nodded. "There is."

"Where is he and what happened to him?" Yagi cocked his head and frowned.

Lee tugged on his arm. "Come on. He's around the next corner. He was unconscious when I left him. Don't even know if he's still breathing."

Yagi followed Lee as they jogged to the far side of the restaurant. "Did somebody shoot the guy?"

"No. I tackled him. We hit the stone wall instead of the floor. His head didn't fare so well."

He rounded the corner and saw the motionless body of the Iranian, his head covered with blood.

Yagi knelt down and checked the man's pulse. "Brandt, next year when the Maui PD takes on the Fire Department in our annual football game, I want you at linebacker." Yagi looked up at Lee. "Well, he's alive...barely." He frowned at Lee again. "Did you blindside him?"

"Close to it. I couldn't afford to give him any warning. He was chasing Jennifer."

Kaai and another officer approached from the direction of the main desk, hearing his words. "Brandt, are you OK? And your wife...she's here? You know that?"

"This Iranian dude needs an ambulance," Officer

Yagi said. "What about your wife?"

"I sent Jennifer up to the fourth floor to hide while I kept these two busy. I need to go up to let her know that I'm OK." *And tell her about Katie.* "If you need me, come up to room 414, Chapel Wing."

"Brandt..." Yagi looked up at him again. "Are you sure there were only two?"

"Only two men chased Jennifer in here. That's all either one of us has seen."

"Kaai, you go with Brandt, just in case," Yagi said.

Lee looked from Yagi to Kaai. "Guys, she was taken on our wedding night. I haven't seen her since then, except when I pushed her into the elevator a few minutes ago. Can we have a few moments alone, please?"

Kaai pushed the elevator button. The door opened. "Sure. As long as I'm convinced it's safe." He motioned towards the elevator door.

Lee stepped inside and pushed number four, and then he shoved everything but Jennifer from his mind, everything except his fearful concern about Katie. He prayed the FBI would get to the yacht in time.

When the two exited the elevator, Lee jogged down the hallway, scanning the room numbers.

"Wait up, Brandt. I don't want you getting into more trouble."

He ignored Kaai and ran to room 414, positioned his face in front of the peephole, and knocked.

The door flew open and Jennifer jumped onto him, locking her arms around his neck and her legs around his waist. Tears spilled from her eyes and splashed onto his neck. "We heard the shots. I was afraid that you—"

"Don't worry, Mrs. Brandt." Kaai chuckled. "Your

husband just sent one of Iranian goons to the hospital. I shot the other one. Just tell me there were only two and I'll leave you two alone for a while."

Jennifer's legs slid down his body and her feet landed on the floor. "Oh. I didn't know anyone was with you. I—" Her cheeks turned rose red.

Lee stepped inside the room and closed the door, leaving Kaai outside. "Now there isn't anyone with me, Jenn." He pulled her lips to his, oblivious to everything but Jennifer.

"Praise the Lord!"

He broke the kiss. "Mrs. Renner, I completely—"

"Yes, you did. But don't stop on my account. I've been praying for you two every hour since last night. Don't I deserve to see the fruits of my labor?"

He kissed her again, but Jennifer hijacked his kiss taking it to an intensity he had never before experienced.

When Jennifer slowly pulled her lips from his, she cupped his cheeks, turned his head, and looked into his eyes. "Finally, we're all safe. There were times when I—"

"Jenn..." His heart ached as he sought words that would be less hurtful, that would soften the blow he had to deal her. Such words didn't exist.

Jennifer's smile faded and turned to a frown. "Lee, what's wrong?"

He pulled her close. "They took Katie. She's on the yacht."

29

Franklin James scanned the blue sky littered with puffy white clouds, looking for any aircraft from Molikini to Maalaea Bay. Only one helicopter. However, the red-orange chopper had flown directly over his yacht twice in the past five minutes.

"Snake, did you tie the girl's feet to the bedpost like I told you?"

"Yes. She won't be rolling around looking for a weapon."

Snake shoved the spear in a storage compartment and turned towards his boss. "You worried about the chopper?"

James rubbed his chin, and then locked gazes with his employee. "What do you make of it?"

Snake gave him a tight-lipped smile. "The Coast Guard is definitely interested in us. That's not good. Means either our million-dollar baby survived and called the cops, or the boat with the snorkelers reported the missing girl. Either way, our time here is limited."

How does one bait a snake? "What do you think the Coast Guard will do?" James studied Snake's face as he waited for a reply.

"This is a hostage situation for them." Snake shrugged. "What else can they do? They'll bring in reinforcements and try to—what is that strategy they teach them at the FBI Academy?"

"The three Cs. Contain, control, and capture. Eventually they'll get to capture. Which probably includes snipers." James looked at the shore, studying it, waiting for Snake to bite.

The lean man followed his gaze. "You're not thinking...No, no way. We're five hundred yards out. They can't—"

"Yes, they can. A sniper with a tactical rifle, say a modified Remington .308, can shoot your eyes out at five hundred yards. At a thousand yards, he can put five consecutive shots in a three-inch circle, such as your forehead." James studied Snake's face again, watching for signs that the man was swallowing the bait.

"Then we'd better stay on the port side by the blonde princess. We'd better not show ourselves on the side facing the shore."

James smiled, not because he agreed with Snake's assessment, but because the snake had slithered through a knothole in the chicken coop and swallowed a golf ball instead of an egg. An old farmer's trick, but it had worked. Snake would never get out of here alive. No one on the yacht would, including the blonde princess.

But I will.

"Mr. James, wouldn't it be better to simply hoist anchor and make a run for the South Pacific?"

"Not an option. The Coast Guard at Oahu just took delivery of their first FRC, Fast Response Cutter. They could outrun us and, with all their firepower, blow us out of the water."

James pointed towards Maalaea. "Look. The Coast Guard is sending both of their boats. It looks like 'contain' is underway."

"Mr. James," Snake's gaze roamed the shore, "Maybe we should all move to the port side now and stay there."

"Go tell Mack," James said. "I'll join you after I talk to the captain."

"I know someone has to take the wheel, but it's a sniper's paradise up there." Snake left for the room where Mack lay resting.

When Snake disappeared from sight, James opened the storage bin by the ladder and moved a small scuba tank, mask, and fins to the front where he could quickly grab them. Then he climbed the stairs to the wheel and warned the captain about sniper fire.

The Amber Alert had created some big challenges. He would probably lose his yacht today, but Franklin James would not die on it, and he refused to spend his life in a federal penitentiary. When everyone else was on the port side, he would grab the air tank, slide into the water, and not surface until he was nearly to Big Beach. If he couldn't steal a car there he would hijack one and drive to the airport where his Gulfstream would take him to Southeast Asia and to safety.

Granted, he would have to take off without permission. Besides being a bit dicey, that would tip off the FBI who, worst case, might scramble fighters from the base on Oahu. But, if he flew towards the southwest at maximum speed, his Gulfstream would be outside the fighter's fuel range before they caught him. When the fighters turned for home, James would be home free.

He smiled. *Great challenges cause great minds to rise to the challenge.*

A few minutes later, James, Snake, and Mack gathered in the cabin next door to the girl. He noted that Mack's neck had stopped bleeding. The man needed some stitches, but he would be OK until..."Mack, do you feel up to watching the girl? As things heat up, we'll need someone with her all the time."

"Yeah. I can handle the girl." Mack's voice was weak and a little hoarse.

"I still haven't heard your plan for getting us out of here." Snake stared at him.

Clearly this was a challenge to his authority and ability. It was unlike Snake to question him. Perhaps James didn't know the man as well as he thought. Perhaps he shouldn't trust the man as much as he had. Perhaps it was another reason Snake should die on the yacht.

James smiled, trying to portray confidence to the men. "We still have a case of dynamite on board and some plastic explosives, don't we?"

His question drew a frown from Snake. "Yes. But how will we—"

"Don't worry, Snake. Desperate times call for desperate measures. Let me take a look outside, tweak my plan a little and then—"

"I'm not going to stay on board if this ship goes down." Snake glared at him.

"You don't have to. It only has to appear that way. Then we all disappear...together. All but the girl. She stays on board." James pounded his fist into his palm. "The princess goes down with the ship."

"But, if anything should go wrong, let's say a sniper picks me off, and then they try to take the ship, put the girl on the deck and let them watch you kill her. Let the whole world watch you kill her."

30

When the man called Snake grabbed Katie's ankles, sliding one on either side of the bedpost and securing them with the restraint, she discarded all of her previous plans to escape. She now lay on her back, hands tied behind her, and her ankles secured to a leg of the bed. This called for a new plan, but in this predicament nothing she could think of seemed to work.

First, she had to free her feet, but freeing her feet required raising the corner of the bed, lifting the bedpost a few inches off the floor. That would allow her to slide the ties around her ankles under the bedpost, permitting her to roll around the room. Even if she accomplished that, it was only step one in a long, risky process that could be upstaged at any moment.

Did they tie Jenn like this? If so, she had managed to escape. But what if they tied Katie like this *because* Jenn had escaped? That was a depressing thought. Nevertheless, Jenn *had* escaped and, somehow, Katie would also.

Could she raise the bed with her back and legs? Katie slid under the bed and tried to roll onto her stomach, so she could pull her knees under her and lift. When she rolled over her legs twisted around each other, tightening the tie around the post. She discarded this approach.

How could she lift while on her back with her

hands tied behind her? The answer was obvious, put her knees on the underside of the bed, instead of on the floor. It might work if she moved under the bed, and then scooted towards the post until her knees were bent upward as far as possible.

Footsteps sounded outside the room. Katie stopped. She lay still, parallel to the bed.

The door opened. A man with an ugly gash on his neck wobbled into the room.

Had Jennifer injured this man?

"I see your wrists aren't bleeding yet." His voice was hoarse. "Maybe our blonde princess is smarter than our million-dollar baby... or a whole lot dumber. After all, you *are* a blonde." The man's hoarse laugh sounded like he was choking. The laugh ended in a coughing spasm that sent him to a chair to recover.

Katie lay on the floor breathing rapidly through her nose. But that was becoming more difficult as her allergies turned her body against itself, narrowing all of her breathing passages.

The man stood after he had recovered. "You're not going anywhere. But I'll be back to check on you, so don't get any ideas." He glared at her. "No one's going to kick me again," he growled as he left the cabin.

So Jennifer *had* injured this man. In so doing, maybe she had made it easier for Katie to disable him.

The cigarette smoke was taking its toll on her entire breathing apparatus. She began wheezing, and that made her grow panicky again. She needed air. She needed to breathe through her mouth. She needed to calm down. She couldn't!

The room seemed to close in on her. She thrashed on the floor as her nose became stuffy from the heavy concentration of smoky allergens.

I can't breathe. I'm going to suffocate!

Though it seemed it might also suffocate her, Katie slid her head under the bed. She raised her head until her cheek pressed into the fabric covering the underside. She tried to rub the tape off from her mouth by twisting her head.

It didn't work. Her breathing turned to rapid panting. Then her nose became blocked. She tried to blow it. That didn't work.

Katie was dizzy. The room spun wildly, out of control. She ground her cheek into the underside of the bed, raised her head using all of her neck strength, and twisted violently, raking her cheek across the fabric.

Skin rasped from her cheek.

No. It was the tape ripping off from her skin. She had snagged a loose corner of the tape.

Now her vision grew gray and fuzzy, as only a small amount of air reached her lungs with each attempt to draw a breath.

Katie's strength drained until it was nearly gone. In desperation, she cocked her head and twisted her neck one last time. The tape peeled off from half her mouth.

She lay on her back gasping, sucking the life-sustaining air of planet Earth into her lungs, and then expelling it as fast as she could through the side of her partially opened mouth.

In a few moments, the room came into focus. Adrenaline still coursed through her veins, but the panic had subsided.

Another twist of her head left the tape stuck to the underside of the bed.

She realized she couldn't have done that on her own, especially after panicking so badly. *I was so scared*

I didn't even think about praying. Thank You for helping me, anyway.

The incident that should've left her in terror seemed, instead, to give her confidence. She wasn't alone in her effort to escape. Katie recalled her plan to use her knees. The plan the injured man had interrupted.

She created a mental picture of how this would work to free her from the bed. Then she slid under the bed and scooted her body directly towards the post which her bound ankles straddled. As she moved closer, her knees bent upward but her feet remained flat on the floor.

When her knees reached their maximum height, she lifted them. The bed raised a couple of inches off from the floor. Unfortunately, her ankles did also.

She couldn't work the restraints under the post to free herself from the bed unless her feet remained on the floor while the corner post raised about four inches. How could she make that happen? She sent another prayer heavenward.

Katie recalled the sit-ups the softball coach made the team do during training. Sit-ups with their knees bent.

Katie tried one and her forehead rose until it pressed hard against the underside of the bed. She tried again. Her forehead and knees together lifted the corner of the bed six inches. Katie put all her strength into the next sit up. As the bed lifted, she scooted her heels towards her rear end. Her feet slid free from the bed post.

When she relaxed from the exertion, the bedpost thumped on the floor. She prayed the noise wouldn't attract attention.

Her relaxation made her aware of the pain coming from the back of her head. It was lying on a hard, uncomfortable object. She slid her upper body out from under the bed, swung her feet around where her head had been, and swept the object out into the light.

It appeared to be half of some ceramic container. A bowl? No, an ashtray. The broken edge looked sharp. Jennifer must have left this. Unknowingly, Jennifer had provided Katie a way of escape.

The sound of a helicopter grew loud, so loud the yacht pulsated with each wop of the rotor. There were voices outside. Someone barked out commands.

The popping of automatic weapons came from the deck. Two or three guns had fired. Then the sound of the helicopter faded. The authorities must be pressuring the people on the yacht.

She was their hostage. Katie knew what this situation meant.

This is when they drag the hostage onto the deck.

She had to hurry. How could she free her hands? First, they had to be in front of her.

Katie rolled onto her knees, extended her long, athletic arms, forced them over her rear end, and then rocked onto her back. She bent her knees to her chest and worked her hands over her feet, one foot at a time.

With her hands in front of her, she grabbed the ceramic shard, jammed it between her feet, and sawed on the wrist restraint. In a few seconds it broke.

The sound of more shots came from outside. Running feet pounded the deck. One set of feet approached her door.

Katie sawed furiously on her ankle restraints. The first one broke.

A man stopped outside her door.

She prayed it was the coughing, injured man.

"I'll get her," the voice hissed.

Not Snake. Please not him.

The last ankle restraint popped in two. Her right hand grabbed the broken ashtray. When she stood, an overstressed calf muscle cramped hard. She didn't need this. Not now.

The door opened partway.

Katie shoved the heel of the cramping leg away from her body, pulling out the charley horse in the process. Her left leg launched her body towards the door.

Snake's skinny head appeared. Its triangular shape reminded Katie of a viper. His eyes widened as Katie's right foot delivered a crushing karate stomp, dead center on the man's face.

His nose flattened. Blood splattered the wall beside the door. Snake grunted and hissed out the dregs of his revolting vocabulary.

Katie gasped when he lunged at her.

31

Lee stroked Jennifer's head. His heart ached for her.

She clung to him. "Lee, they can't have Katie. I won't let them have Katie. I'll—"

He lifted her chin and kissed her forehead. "Let's pray that God and Katie won't let them have Katie."

"I'm on it." Bertha Renner's intense voice came from across the room.

"Thank you," Jennifer said as she choked back a sob. "But I've got to know how Katie is."

Lee shook his head. "We probably can't find out right now. But if Granddad is still in the rented boat he—"

"I've got to know *something*." Her pleading brown eyes ripped at Lee's heart. "Call him, Lee. Please."

Before he could pull his cell from the pocket of his cargo shorts, it rang. He knew who it was before looking at the caller ID. He checked it anyway for Jennifer's sake. "It's Granddad."

He put the cell to his ear. "Lee, is she OK?" Granddad's excited voice sounded loudly above the idling boat motors in the background.

"She's standing beside me, and she's fine."

"What about the Iranians?"

"One was shot. The other has head injuries. They're both in police custody and on the way to the hospital."

"Lee, what did you do? Probably more than you should have."

"I didn't do much. Delayed until the police—"

Jennifer snatched his cell. "He saved my life, Granddad. We're in the room of the woman who saw me abducted and started the Amber Alert, Mrs. Renner. But we want to know about Katie. What's happening on the yacht?"

The sound of the boat motors died. Jennifer turned on the cell's speakerphone.

"There are two Coast Guard boats here, a police boat, two helicopters, and the shore is lined with police. They made me move away, about a mile to the north. But I've got Lee's high-power binoculars."

Granddad didn't answer Jennifer's question, not directly, and he made no mention of Katie. Lee wasn't sure how to read that, but avoiding Jennifer's question was *not* a good sign.

"Have you seen Katie?" Jennifer had cut to the chase. Evidently her patience was gone.

"No," Granddad said. "I haven't seen Katie. But I think I know where she is. The second cabin on the port side. I've seen men go in and come out. But since the authorities made me move my boat, I can't see that side of the yacht."

"That's the room where they put me. Katie won't tolerate it very well. It's a smoker's room. This isn't good." Her twin frown lines deepened.

Lee leaned close to the phone. "Granddad, tell us what the boats and the choppers are doing. At some point the authorities will give the goons an ultimatum, then move in if they don't surrender."

Granddad's sigh was audible through the phone. "The goons, as you called them, haven't surrendered. I heard a few gunshots. Then one helicopter backed off. But three of the boats are moving closer now. I saw some strange weapons on two of the boats. Scary looking weapons."

Jennifer's body grew rigid. "But they'll try to negotiate Katie's release first, won't they?"

Lee was certain Jennifer knew the ground rules for a hostage situation. They would order them to release Katie. It would be an ultimatum with little room for negotiation. Unless Katie's captors wanted to dialogue and indicated they wanted to avoid a gun battle, the scary looking weapons would probably be turned on the yacht.

Since the traffickers had already fired on the chopper, the "capture" scenario could be implemented at any moment.

"Another police boat has moved into position. On the back side of the boat, hidden from the yacht, three men wearing tanks just entered the water." Granddad's voice lost its usual calmness.

Men in the water. Men like Navy SEALs? Maybe "capture" included a plan to rescue Katie.

"Jenn, we need to pray for Katie. Now."

Her eyes widened. "Come on. Let's go down to the beach before—"

"I'm not sure they'll let us on the beach. It's too near the yacht. Besides, we don't have binoculars. We wouldn't be able to see anything."

"There's an observation area in the hotel. You can see everything for miles." Mrs. Renner smiled when he and Jennifer turned towards her. "And I have a pair of binoculars. Brought them for whale watching." She opened the guest guide for the Grand Wailea Resort and turned to a diagram of the facility. "The observation area is right here."

Jennifer grabbed the binoculars Bertha Renner had fished out of her beach bag. "Thanks. Let's go, Lee. I need to see. I need to know."

"Granddad, Jenn and I are moving to an observation deck in the resort. We have binoculars. We'll call you in a bit. Pray for Katie. Bye."

Jennifer hooked his arm and pulled him towards the door. "Thanks again for taking me in and for your prayers, Mrs. Renner."

"Honey, it was no problem. Now you go help them find your little girl, and I'll continue to pray."

Lee and Jenn ran as soon as they were out the door.

From the observation deck, they could see the whole drama unfolding. But Bertha Renner's binoculars were wide-angle, for sighting whales. They weren't high powered. The panorama they could see well. But the small details were hidden by the distance.

While Jennifer trained the binoculars on the yacht, Lee visually scanned the shoreline near Wailea Point. For three or four hundred yards, the beach was cordoned off. On the point, he saw two men with sniper's rifles. "Capture" was cocked and aimed. Lee prayed that the Coast Guard, Peterson, and the Maui Police Department had planned well, and that they had given Katie a chance to survive what was coming in the next few minutes.

32

Over the past five minutes, the boats surrounding his yacht had drawn closer. Two helicopters flew a tight circle around them. Franklin James pulled the binoculars to his eyes and peered through a small crack towards Wailea Point. Two men with rifles. Snipers.

He moved to the port side. The police boat was only four hundred yards away. He stepped into the doorway of the cabin where the others had congregated, turned towards the police boat, and focused his binoculars on it.

"Snipers!" James yelled the word and dropped to the deck.

Chaos broke out in the cabin as Snake, Mack, and the Captain dove to the floor near the back wall.

James slammed the cabin door behind him, crawled to the storage bin, snagged the diving gear with one hand, and gently rolled off the deck. After grabbing the ladder with his free hand, he swung his legs downward to the ladder. He took two quick steps down the ladder then jumped into the water.

As he sank into the warm blue water, he ripped off his shoes and started the air flowing. He cleared the water from the hose and slid his lips over the mouthpiece. The closed-circuit rebreather would give him three hours if he needed it, and with the water cleared, this apparatus would produce no telltale bubbles.

He pulled on the mask and cleared it, then slipped on the fins. Using the orientation of the yacht thirty feet above him, he turned to the south and began swimming towards Makena Point. The large parking lot at the hotel there would provide a better selection of vehicles than Big Beach, and he could reach it ten minutes sooner. Each minute he gained improved his chances of getting away safely.

To move faster, James turned westward to pick up the current in the channel between the islands. Though it lay one hundred yards out of his way, the channel current would add one or two miles per hour to his swimming speed.

As he moved through the water, James began to work on his biggest problem, getting both his pilot and himself on board his Gulfstream without getting caught. The pieces of a plan began falling into place and he focused entirely on completing it.

A movement to his left caught his eye. A large tiger shark was feeding on a sea turtle. The big fish left its meal and darted towards him. James sucked a gasp of air from the tank but had no time to react.

The menacing creature glided past him in the water. One cold, staring eye seemed to lock his gaze for a moment. When the shark turned towards him again, James prepared for the futile attempt to defend himself against a fish designed to be a killing machine. But today, at this moment, the shark preferred sea turtle to Franklin James.

He shook uncontrollably as he swam southward, putting as much distance between himself and those tooth-lined jaws as he could.

He was Franklin James, too intelligent and careful to be nervous. It was a lie he had told himself until he almost believed it. Then a million-dollar girl with an IQ of two hundred had slipped through his fingers, made a fool of him, and he was forced to flee underwater to save his life, a life that lay completely at the mercy, or whims, or appetite, whatever drove the deadly jaws of a tiger shark.

For a brief moment, James wondered if that was how the girls he kidnapped felt when they realized their situation was hopeless, like they were at the mercy of a shark. But with the shark out of sight, the sympathy for the many girls he had sold into slavery faded until it disappeared. Franklin James returned to what he had chosen to become, a modern-day slaver who didn't believe in sympathy, didn't believe in grace, and didn't believe in God. A man who believed only in himself.

He surfaced briefly, faced the Makena Beach Resort, dove, and swam hard towards his destination.

****

Lee pulled Jennifer close to his side while they watched the Coast Guard and police boats move into position to take the yacht. Like the timer on a bomb, the countdown to the capture ticked inexorably towards an explosion of violence.

Obviously the human traffickers were not going to surrender. If they brought Katie out as a shield for bargaining, he would take Jennifer off the observation deck. Knowing Katie was in the clutches of these men already stressed Jennifer to her limits. He couldn't let her watch if...

With binoculars pressed against her face, Jennifer's gaze swung towards one of the police boats. "Lee, they're firing on the yacht."

"That's because the yacht's crew hoisted anchor. Looks like they want to make a run for it." It wasn't good. No matter how he sliced it, the situation meant more danger for Katie.

"The windows by the wheel of the boat just shattered."

"Makes sense," Lee said. "They may have raised the anchor, but the yacht's captain can't steer the boat without getting shot. They're not going anywhere."

Jennifer spun the fine focus adjustment. "The gunfire has all the goons pinned down. I can see the three divers now. They're armed and moving along the starboard side of the deck, clearing each cabin as they pass."

"But Katie and the goons are on the other side. When they hoisted the anchor, the ship turned. We won't be able to see what happens on the port side."

"At the corner I see someone. It looks like Snake, firing an assault rifle. Can't tell what he's shooting at. He kicked a box sitting on the deck. It looks like he's sliding it to a spot on the starboard side. It's total chaos on the yacht."

"Here comes—check the Coast Guard boat on the west side of the yacht. What kind of weapon is—"

"It's a machine gun. A big one and—Lee, an explosion on the yacht!"

She lowered the binoculars and buried her face in his chest. "Please, Lord, save Katie from this."

Lee echoed Jennifer's prayer softly and then sought words to comfort her. "Katie's no ordinary fifteen-year-old. She's extremely bright and she's strong. You escaped and she's a lot stronger physically than you."

Jennifer lifted her head from his chest and looked towards the yacht.

A second explosion painted orange flames over the entire yacht. Large pieces of the ship flew in all directions, littering the water with burning debris just as the deep boom reached them.

"No one could survive that. No one." Her voice became soft, resigned, and her sobbing began.

The SEALS, or whoever the divers were, had bailed seconds before the boat exploded. He saw three heads bobbing in the water, and then all three submerged.

Four boats moved in close to the yacht. One began shooting an arc of water onto the burning yacht.

It was far too little and much too late. At best, Lee thought, they might prevent the yacht from sinking. If so, they could start forensics as soon as it was safe. Would they find Katie's body charred into an unrecognizable corpse? Would it be riddled with bullet holes?

He had to stop this kind of speculation or lose his mind.

Jennifer sobbed against his chest.

And now his own tears dripped down and mingled with hers.

Their Maui honeymoon had turned into a nightmare last night. Would that now include a funeral? A funeral for one of the most beautiful and brightest young women he had ever known? The girl who was supposed to become their daughter?

33

Katie sucked in a short breath of air when Snake's body went airborne. The coiled snake had struck from nearly ten feet away. His body darted toward her. Instinctively she squeezed the ceramic shard and flung her right arm back into throwing position. She had no time. Couldn't wind up. Katie threw from the stretch. Her trained arm, now enhanced by adrenaline, cracked like a whip.

She delivered a fastball down the middle of the plate. A pitch much faster than any she had ever thrown. Katie pushed backward, backpedaling as she watched her throw hit its mark between Snakes beady, lifeless eyes.

A crack sounded like a baseball meeting a bat, like an extra-base hit. Blood exploded from Snake's brow. He dropped to the floor at Katie's feet. Snake made no sound. But best of all, he didn't move.

She leapt over his body towards the cabin door, but the shockwave from an explosion hit her head like a club. Flames shot past the cabin door.

Katie shook off the dazed feeling, leaped through the residual flames from the explosion, and drew a deep breath as she dove over the railing. When she cleared it, she saw Mack step out of the adjacent cabin. He held an assault rifle.

The brief sting of flames was extinguished when her five-foot-nine frame slid into the warm water. She pulled hard for the bottom.

Pain! Excruciating pain came from two hammer-like blows to her back. Katie writhed in the water then felt for the spots on her back.

When she turned her head to look through the clear water at her back, a small object tumbled from her body and sank towards the bottom, then disappeared into the darkness below her. No blood. Thank God. Mack had shot her with the assault rifle. She sent another silent prayer of thanks heavenward for the outcome.

If she had been only three or four feet under, she would be either dead or dying. But somewhere between eight and ten feet below the surface, she received only painful bruises. Bruises showing she had been protected, protected by the God she was learning to trust more deeply every day.

Each time Katie kicked her legs, pain exploded across her lower back, but she couldn't stop until the oxygen from her last breath was completely used up. Swimming ten feet under the surface, Katie pulled hard for shore, praying there would be no more gunfire. At the end of her breath, she rose to the uncertain welcome awaiting her at the surface.

****

Lee's gaze moved from the scene of destruction in the water to Jennifer's tear-streaked face.

She stepped close to him, her large brown eyes pleading for help. "Whatever the news, good or bad, I need to know something. Call Peterson, Lee. The crisis is over now. He should be willing to talk to us."

Lee studied her eyes, her face, her body posture.

"Are you sure? Can you handle—"

"Yes. Call. Now." She closed her eyes and pressed her cheek into his chest. "Please."

Lee drew a deep breath, steeling his mind for the worst, and pressed Peterson's number on his speed dial. The call went directly to his voicemail. "He's probably on the line."

"Then wait about thirty seconds and call again. You can't stop calling until you've reached him." Jennifer blinked back tears. "I've cried until I can't cry anymore, prayed until I can't think of anything else to pray for, and I can't stand this waiting. Please, try Peterson again."

For the second time, Lee went through the process of preparing his mind and body for the call, then dialed.

Peterson answered on the second ring. "Lee, I was going to call you when we had the situation under—"

"Did you find Katie?" He pressed the button turning on his speaker phone, praying it wasn't a mistake.

"We found evidence that Katie was on board, but we didn't find her, and it looks like—"

"She was in the second cabin on the port side. That's where they put me."

"Is that you, Jennifer?"

"Yes. Did you check that cabin?"

"That's where we found the evidence. It's also where we found the remains of a tall skinny guy. It appears his nose had been hit hard and he had a deep gash on his forehead. He evidently laid there and partially burned, so we think he was unconscious. I've seen Katie in action. She might have disabled him. One other thing, we didn't find the ring leader, James."

Lee was encouraged by both Peterson's news and the excitement growing in Jennifer's eyes.

Jennifer leaned close to Lee's cell. "Maybe Katie hit him with the ceramic ashtray that I broke and used to cut my restraints. I slashed another man's neck with it when I escaped."

"We did find something that sounds like a piece of your ashtray." Peterson paused. "From where it lay in the cabin, it probably was the weapon. But I don't see how Katie could have—"

"Peterson..." Lee interrupted. "I've seen Katie throw a baseball over eighty miles per hour. If she was afraid and fighting for her life, she might've sent a ninety mile per hour fastball into that guy's—"

"Snake. Into Snake's face." Jennifer sounded breathless, and excitement filled her voice. "Lee, she got away! The same way that I did. Katie got away."

"We've been combing the water around the yacht, but no signs of Katie." Peterson heaved a heavy sigh. "So I'm not—"

"She can swim," Lee said. "A lot faster than me. That's how she got into trouble in the first place."

"Then she'll head for shore. But right after the explosion, I saw shooting on the yacht." Jennifer's frown returned. "We've got to find her soon. She may be hurt. She would swim for shore, like I did."

"Swim to shore, yes. But perhaps not like you did. Thanks, Peterson. Please let us know if you find out more."

Lee ended the call and cupped Jennifer's cheek. "I'm going to call Granddad and ask him to turn in the boat and drive down to meet us here. In the meantime, we can run the beach trail and see if Katie swims ashore near us. But I've got a feeling she would swim further south, maybe towards the Makena Beach Resort."

"You mean because of the way the yacht was turned when she escaped?"

"Exactly. When the chaos broke out on the yacht, just before the shooting and explosions, the yacht's port side was facing the southwest. If she looked towards shore, she would have been looking at Makena Point, near the Makena Beach Resort."

Jennifer's dark eyebrows nearly touched.

Her intense frown, after looking so hopeful, got his attention. "What is it? Jenn, you need to tell me what you're thinking."

She met his gaze. "If James escaped, it would have been near the same time as Katie. He probably would swim towards the Makena Beach Resort, too. He would need a car to get to the airport and a plane to leave the island."

"Are you thinking he might also need a hostage?"

Jennifer nodded. "Lee, we can't let that man take Katie again. Call Granddad and tell him to meet us out at the street. We need to get to Makena Point now."

34

The urge to breathe mushroomed out of control. Katie's head broke the surface. The bright sun blinded her. Her chest heaved spasmodically as she tried to pay a seemingly insurmountable oxygen debt.

She would be here for several seconds recovering, so she swiveled in the water and looked back at the yacht. Flames ravaged the entire ship. Could anyone on it still be alive? What had happened?

One thing was clear. The timing of her escape had been impeccable. Only an all-knowing God who loved her could orchestrate an escape so precise amid total chaos and pulse-pounding panic. Her trust for the One who loved her grew to new heights.

With the entire yacht burning, no one would be shooting at her now. Even if someone were alive on the yacht, their chief concern would be remaining so.

Still, no sense taking unnecessary risks. She had come too far. Katie took three more deep breaths and submerged, swimming underwater towards the V-shaped resort beside a hill that resembled a miniature volcano.

Had it been fifteen minutes or an hour? Katie had no idea as she stumbled up the beach towards the resort. Small waves slapped at her backside. One reached high enough to slap the bruises on her back.

The pain reminded her of her incredible escape. She had been shot by an assault rifle and had survived.

She couldn't wait to tell Granddad, to see his face. He would be horrified, but then his smile, one that could span the width of his entire face, would replace his wide eyes. Like her, he would give thanks to the God he had recently begun to trust.

The resort lay a hundred yards up the hill. Numerous concrete walkways traversed the grassy grounds surrounding the building. She took the one that led most directly to an entry point.

The sidewalk hurt her bare feet. Katie stepped to the side of the rough concrete and ran on the grass. To her right someone was doing exactly what she was, jogging on the grass. She looked more closely and stopped, frozen by fear.

She was staring at James.

He returned her stare.

Somehow he had escaped, probably leaving his men to die. But he wouldn't want her to testify to that or to a dozen other atrocities she could attribute to the man.

Katie looked ahead to the entrance nearest her. It was seventy or eighty yards away. She sprinted towards it with all the speed her strong legs could generate.

Halfway to the building, she glanced back. James was a tenderfoot, at least that's what his gait told her. She pulled away from him. With a lead of fifty yards, Katie flew through the entryway and turned up a large corridor that ran towards what she hoped was the front desk, towards people, towards phones, and hopefully towards security guards.

Katie rounded a corner and ran up to a large counter. The young man behind the counter stared at a monitor and pecked on a keyboard.

Thirty feet away, Katie began her plea for help. "Call 911, I'm one of the captives from the yacht. I escaped, but the head of the gang is only a few seconds behind me."

She had the young man's attention, but he stood frowning, making no move to help.

James turned the corner, thirty yards away.

"There he is. Call 911 now!"

The clerk finally reached for the phone.

She had only a moment to decide what to do. James was already close enough to kill her if he had a gun. Trying to run away could hasten that.

An image of a training session with Granddad flashed through her mind. She decided to try in the real world what she had only rehearsed in practice.

As James bore down on her, Katie feigned wide-eyed fear that froze her to the spot. She didn't need to fake the fear, only the freezing part. It wasn't easy because every impulse her panicky mind gave her was to run, run to the left, to the right, run anywhere, but not to remain here.

James slowed as he approached her. His dead eyes met her gaze, and his arms reached for her. His fingers spread wide to grab her shoulders or arms.

Katie recalled his strong hand clamping on her arm when he lifted her onto the yacht. She couldn't let him get a grip on her.

With determination in his eyes and on his face, James rushed at her.

Katie planted her left foot behind her and, in an explosion of energy, kicked her right foot into James's onrushing face.

He hadn't a clue the kick was coming. Her powerful leg drove his head backward while his feet continued towards her. James went down hard on his back. Blood splattered from his nose, and his head struck the floor with a loud sound that would surely be accompanied by pain.

How much pain? Katie didn't know, so she couldn't rely on a single kick stopping a man as strong and desperate as James.

Flat on his back on the floor, James raised his head.

Katie stomped his solar plexus as Granddad had demonstrated.

The air rushed from his lungs. He tried to suck the air back in. It was a vain attempt.

Her kick had done its intended work.

James's head flopped back onto the floor.

Knocking the breath out of him would only temporarily incapacitate him. Katie drove her fist into his exposed throat, dead center on his larynx.

James clutched his throat, thrashing wildly as he fought to breathe. Either his breathing would eventually return, or he would die shortly without medical help.

Katie hadn't a clue how much damage she had done. But James would be, according to Granddad, incapacitated for two or three minutes at a minimum and perhaps forever.

Katie turned to look over the counter at the young man.

He stood holding the phone, mouth open, eyes wide.

"Did you call 911?" Katie's voice was loud, demanding. She stepped towards him.

"Yes." With his gaze locked on her, the young man backed away.

"Do you have security guards in the building?"

"Yes." The young man took another step backward.

"Call them, now. Before he recovers."

In her peripheral vision two people appeared running towards her. Katie tensed at this new danger. She turned towards them in a fighting posture.

"Katie!"

It was Jennifer and Lee.

Jennifer's arms wrapped around her. Love and security flowed in, and Katie relaxed for the first time in nearly a day.

Lee squeezed her shoulder but turned immediately to the prostrate man making choking noises on the floor. "Is this James?" Lee's gaze darted between Katie and the man.

"That's him," Jennifer answered.

Katie nodded and then glared at the incapacitated man.

****

Lee surveyed the area around them and then looked over the counter into a small room behind it. "Grab the five iron out of that golf bag."

The clerk didn't move.

Lee glared at the young man behind the counter. "Get it now, dude, or this guy is going to get up again."

The guy stood frozen.

Lee pointed a thumb at the man on the floor. "Would you like some of what this guy got?"

Katie turned towards the clerk and raised her right fist.

"I'm on it." The clerk pulled the five iron from the

golf bag and gingerly handed it to Lee.

Lee yanked it from the man's hand and swiveled towards James, who was making feeble attempts to stand as he choked down inadequate amounts of air.

Granddad trotted in from the entrance and ran straight for Katie. "Thank God, Katie, I was so worried about you."

With Granddad's arms around her, Katie's tears of relief began to flow. She choked off a sob. "Granddad, you saved my life."

"But how? I wasn't even—"

"The kick, the stomp, and the throat punch." Katie smiled through her tears.

"You delivered all three...to him?" He pointed at the man clutching his throat.

"I had to. We evidently both swam from the yacht to the same spot. He saw me, chased me in here, and I tried to surprise him. I didn't know what else to do. I was so scared."

Granddad's arms were around her again. "I think you did all the right things, Katie. That was all the self-defense I had time to teach you. No, I won't scold you for the throat punch. This"—Granddad pointed towards James with a look of disgust—"is what the throat punch was meant for."

Katie winced and gasped when Granddad's arm pressed on her bruises.

"Katie, are you hurt? What happened?" Jennifer moved close to her.

Katie hesitated. "They shot me, sort of."

"Shot you?" Jennifer's eyes widened. "Where?"

"In the back. Actually all across my back, but I was about eight feet under water. The bullets didn't penetrate. They only gave me bruises."

"Let me check your back." Jennifer spun her around. "Deep bruises. Two of them. Both are on muscles. We should have a doctor look at them. Sometimes deep-tissue trauma can cause problems."

Lee draped an arm around Katie and glanced at Granddad who stood watch over James.

"Jenn, take my cell and call Peterson. Would you please? I've got a daughter to attend to."

Katie stretched her tear-stained cheeks and formed a smile.

He pulled her close. This young lady who had saved his life twice in the past six weeks continued to amaze him with her incredible ability to come through in a crisis.

"Katie," he whispered in her ear, "maybe you should consider that offer Peterson gave you a few weeks ago. He'll probably offer it again when he sees this." Lee gestured towards James.

Jennifer handed Lee his cell phone. "Peterson is on his way. I could hear the relief in his voice. But we'll probably all have to endure a lecture, complete with all sorts of threats, when he gets here."

Sirens grew louder and tires screeched to a stop in the parking area behind the resort.

Lee released Katie and glanced at James. His coughing and choking had subsided. He locked gazes with the man. This guy was desperate. With the police arriving, he would test Granddad. Lee opened his mouth to warn him.

James rolled away from Granddad and pushed himself up from the floor. Granddad's whirling kick put the man on the floor again.

"That was only a warning. If you move again, I'll kill you." Granddad's voice held an icy chill that Lee found intimidating even though it wasn't directed at him.

He studied Granddad's face and posture. Everything about him at the moment was intimidating, despite his age and his size.

"He's not listening, Granddad," Katie said. "Look at his eyes. You need to—"

James rolled towards Granddad this time and tried to snag a leg.

A leap and a stomp stilled James. The man appeared to be out cold.

Two uniformed men came to a stop nearby with their guns out. One of them addressed the clerk. "Who are the good guys and who are the bad ones?"

The clerk pointed down at James. "He's the bad dude. But that little guy standing over him is one bad dude, too. And the girl," he shook his head and whistled, "She's something else. Took this guy out all by herself. To look at her you'd think—"

Katie's glare cut off the clerk's statement.

Lee locked gazes with the nearest officer. "The guy on the floor is named James. The leader of the gang on the yacht. He just got his bell rung, twice."

"By,"—the officer pointed at Granddad, then at Katie—"you two?"

"Most recently by my Granddad." Katie smiled at the policeman. "We warned him, but he wouldn't listen, so Granddad kicked the devil out of him."

Lee draped an arm around Katie. "With him, Katie," he nodded towards James. "I don't think it's possible to kick him *that* hard. But then I'm not the man's judge."

The officer smiled at Katie. "I'd better read him his rights so he can eventually face someone who is."

35

Lee looked across the hotel lobby towards the entryway when a tall man wearing a suit entered. Peterson had arrived. Following him were two Maui police officers.

"The place is already crawling with news media. Microphones, cameras, vans, even a helicopter from Channel 7 on Oahu. They swarm to violence like a shark to blood in the water." Peterson shook his head. "You'd think these people have never seen a yacht explode and burn before." He cracked a grin as he strode up to Katie and Jennifer. "Are you two all right?"

Jennifer let out a sharp sigh. "We thought so, but they shot Katie in the back while—"

"Shot her!" Peterson's voice boomed out, echoing down the hallway.

"I dove into the water and the bullets from—I think it was an AK-47—bounced off my back. They just bruised me."

"Bruised you?" Peterson took a calming breath. He held Katie's gaze and shook his head. "Do you want me to tell you what the odds of that are, young lady?"

"It doesn't matter. Odds never matter with God." Katie smiled.

"You may be right about that, Katie, but we still should have you looked at. Deep muscle bruising can have complications."

"Yeah. That's what Jenn told me."

Peterson looked at the clerk behind the counter. "Do you have a doctor on duty here?"

"Yes, sir. Until 8:00 PM this evening."

"Call him."

The young man didn't move.

Peterson flipped out his badge. "I'm Special Agent Peterson, FBI and I'm the Incident Commander for the entire operation involving the yacht and the abduction. I want this young lady to see a doctor now."

Startled, the young man reached for the phone.

"He's a little slow." Lee chuckled. "But not a bad kid."

"I'm not slow." The clerk glared at Lee. "My IQ is 125 and I—"

"Sorry, buddy. Katie's got you beat by forty points and Jennifer"—he nodded towards her—"by eighty. No offense. Slow's just a relative thing." Lee grinned at him.

"Good grief. What kind of people are you? A bunch of geniuses who can kick like Chuck Norris, but look like..." his gaze darted between Katie and Jennifer.

"Like the cream of the crop." Lee smiled at the young man. "Meet my wife and my daughter."

"But she's not old enough to have a child her age and," he pointed to Katie, "she's too old to be your—"

"Kid, you're digging a hole for yourself. If you tick Katie off she'll—"

"Yeah, I know. Tick rhymes with kick."

"The doctor..." Peterson pointed to the phone in the clerk's hand.

"I'm on it, sir." The young man nodded.

****

Lee held Jennifer's hand. He glanced at her face. The hand was attached to a body that was incredibly beautiful. But best of all, it was alive. Maybe the nightmare was over.

As the five walked towards the doctor's office, Katie move from Jennifer's side and took a position beside the tall FBI agent. "Does the offer you made to me six weeks ago still stand?"

"Does that mean you might give the bureau try?"

Katie sighed sharply. "It's a lot more than might." She paused. "You're not going to be retired in five years are you?"

Peterson chuckled. "I don't plan to, but why—"

"I'm starting college early. I should graduate when I'm twenty, in about four and a half years. I just wondered if—"

"Yes, I'll be around...as you say, Lord willing. And I'd be delighted to be a reference for you, Katie. The bureau could never have enough like you."

"She sure beats Bastian," Lee quipped.

"I didn't give *him* a reference." Peterson sighed. "I just got saddled with the young guy who was a square peg in a round hole. Now let's see what the doctor has to say."

Lee watched the doctor motion for Katie to step into a small examination room.

When the door closed, Jennifer looked up at the tall FBI agent. "There are some things I need to know."

He looked down at her. "Shoot. I'll help if I can."

"As you know, this is our second attempt to...to...I don't want to spend my wedding night worrying about uninvited guests." Her voice rose in volume and in pitch.

"Don't worry, Jennifer. We got them all. They'll never bother you again. You've got my word on it."

"Not good enough, Peterson. I need to have an accounting. What about the guy called Cookie?"

"Cookie. He was shot by one of his own gang members a couple of hours ago."

"There was another guy...I called him Mao. I never knew his name, but he had a Chinese accent. He was at the house in Kihei."

"He's the guy who shot Cookie. We don't know if Cookie will survive, but he talked a little. As a result, we got Mao—his real name is Nguyen—near the airport, about an hour ago. He was James's pilot for his Gulfstream."

"Then that only leaves one more." She looked at Peterson and frowned.

He shrugged. "I've already told you about all the gang members who weren't killed on the yacht. Well, all except Anya, who we have in custody."

Jennifer's eyes reached their laser-like intensity. "What about the prince?"

Peterson winced at the name.

"Peterson, he was going to buy me. His boat had nearly docked against the yacht when I dove overboard. I want to know about the prince."

Lee had been on the receiving end of Jennifer's laser look enough times to know how Peterson felt. But the question she asked was a fair one, and he wanted to hear a straight answer, too.

"The prince. Unfortunately, he is treated by our State Department as if he has diplomatic immunity."

Jennifer glared at him and opened her mouth to speak.

Peterson continued. "Don't take your frustration out on me. I don't agree with that policy, but his country, his stature there, and his wealth have won him the right to commit unspeakable crimes against Americans and a lot of other people."

"The right? No one is granted the right to do what he does." Jennifer clenched her jaw.

Peterson met her glaring gaze. "They are when people forget the real source of their rights. But, Jennifer, he won't bother you tonight. He flew home on his private plane. Actually, he took his Dash 8 from Lahaina to Oahu and is now on his Gulfstream headed home. Empty-handed…this time."

Jennifer balled her fists. "When does it stop?" She spat the words at Peterson.

"I don't know. We need an outcry, more voices, stronger voices. The best thing you can do is write up your story along with your complaint and send it to the Department of Justice and the State Department. Then call a conservative news network and tell them you'll give them an exclusive interview if they're interested in your story. You can bet they'll be more than interested, especially if you give them a picture of yourself." Peterson grinned. "You'll be placing yourself at the center of a controversy, but that will also guarantee the prince won't bother you again."

"Yes. I can see why he wouldn't try to take me again. But would he have me killed? And what about other girls? He'll continue taking—"

"Have you killed? I doubt that. He's more into using women than killing them. Taking other girls? Yes, Jennifer, he probably will. But I can give you his MO. He throws big parties in big cities and spreads the word that big name producers and modeling firms will be there. He attracts beautiful young women, makes his choice, drugs them, and they disappear. If you tell that to enough people, maybe his parties won't have any guests."

"I'll do that. But it isn't enough." She shook her head.

Peterson drew a deep breath and blew it back out. "This trafficking business is ugly whether it's done by a dealer like James or consumer like the prince. As long as there are consumers, the trafficking will continue. For now we have to chase the dealers to other countries and make it so hot for consumers that they stop consuming in the US."

"If I attack the prince in the media, will he send someone after me?"

"He never has done that. Not that we know of. But Jennifer—"

"I know. You can't promise he won't." She paused. "Thanks for being honest with me."

"You're welcome. You're a strong, brave young woman. I've seen it many times over the past nine months. I'll do whatever I can to help if you decide to declare war on him."

She turned to Lee. "It's a decision you and I will have to make together." She stepped close to Lee. "But the prince can wait."

Peterson struck up a conversation with Granddad.

Jennifer turned her attention to Lee.

"Let's forget about last night. It shouldn't count. We can make tonight our one and only wedding night." She leaned her head on his shoulder.

"I wouldn't want anyone to know how we spent the night after our wedding."

Peterson turned away from his conversation with

Granddad and back towards Jennifer and Lee.

She continued. "Spending most of the night tied up on the bedroom floor, I—"

"Look," Peterson frowned. "What you to do in private is your own business, but I don't want to hear about it."

Jennifer's cheeks glowed red. "Lee, say something."

"Why? I think he made his feelings on the matter perfectly clear."

Peterson rolled his eyes. "Changing the subject…"

"Please do." Jennifer moved her face behind Lee's shoulder.

"To be safe, I'm assigning a couple of officers to you two, at least for tonight. When we told the Maui PD about this assignment, two police officers volunteered for the night duty. Demanded it be given to them. What's that all about, Lee?"

"I don't know. Who are they?"

"Officers Yagi and Kaai."

He grinned. "They pulled their guns on me the last night. Maybe they're feeling bad about that."

"Lee, you didn't tell me anything about guns." Jennifer gave him a frowning stare.

"I'll tell you about it later. At least I'll know the two officers who'll be watching us tonight."

"Watching us?" Jennifer's eyebrows pinched until they nearly touched. "Please tell me you meant that in a figurative sense."

"Of course I did. We couldn't have them seeing you tied up on the floor."

36

Lee's stomach grumbled and his mouth watered at the delightful smells of grilled chicken, peppers, and spices emanating from the taqueria's kitchen. Katie, Jennifer, and Granddad sat around the table with him, apparently caught up in the music of a talented guitarist who could also sing.

The sun beamed in from the west, reaching into the alcove housing the restaurant. As far as he knew, none of them had eaten since breakfast. The day hadn't allowed them to focus on bodily needs, except for one: staying alive. He looked at Jennifer. *Or keeping someone you love alive.*

Jennifer placed her hand over his and drew his gaze. "Why do you suppose all this happened to us?" She squinted and frowned. "Were we supposed to learn something?"

Lee averted her gaze again and looked down at the floor. "Supposed to? I'm not sure. But I did learn something."

She cupped his cheek and pulled his face towards hers.

He looked into her eyes. "I learned that even when I hate what's happening, I can trust Him." He paused. "When it's me that's dying, I've always been able to say, even if He kills me, I will still trust Him. But when it's people I love who may die..." He caressed her cheek. "My trust grew weak. It vanished. I'm just a—"

"Don't say it, Lee. It's not true."

He looked away.

"Look at me." She pulled his head around to face her. "Do you trust Him right now?"

"More than ever."

"Then it's OK." She smiled warmly, approvingly. "Me, too."

Katie leaned towards them and placed her hand over Jennifer's. "Me, three."

Granddad nodded. "You can count me in."

Katie glanced from Lee to Jennifer. "And I'm going to trust Him to give me a new sister very soon."

Jennifer's cheeks turned rose red. "Katie, there are *some* things…"

Katie's cheeks turned pink. "I was talking about Anya. I think she's a seeker, and I'm praying she'll become a believer. About a baby sister…I'll leave that up to you and Lee."

Lee caught her gaze. "Yes, please do."

Katie's cheeks turned a brighter shade of pink, and she looked down at her blue cover up. She raised her head slowly and smiled at Jennifer. "Thanks for buying the swimsuit cover-up for me. Even though this is Maui, I was beginning to feel a little conspicuous running around in my two-piece swimsuit."

"Yeah," Lee grinned, "You should feel conspicuous the way that clerk at the hotel looked at you once he realized you weren't going for his Adam's apple."

Katie sighed and her normal color returned. She glanced from him to Jennifer to Granddad. "The doctor said I was fine. Everybody is safe. We all trust God even more than we did before. So, what's next?"

Jennifer took Katie's hand. "What is next? If you

think you'd like it, what's next is swimming in this water at a more leisurely pace. On top, not underneath, and with someone like…say…Jess."

Katie's eyes widened and the corners of her mouth turned up. "I get to see your sisters? Are you serious?"

"Yes." Jennifer returned her smile.

"I'd love it." Her smile faded. "I never got to travel, you know, before. I don't think I've ever been out of Western Washington until yesterday."

"You don't fly three thousand miles across the Pacific and spend only a few hours." Granddad smiled at his great-granddaughter.

Jennifer squeezed her hand. "We wouldn't want you to waste the airfare."

Lee nodded. "Jennifer and I will call your school first thing in the morning and—"

"No." Granddad met Lee's gaze. "I will call the school. You and Jennifer have better things to do. You do remember my stipulation when I approved your courtship?"

"About wanting great-grandchildren?" Jennifer's eyes widened.

Granddad nodded.

Katie looked at the glances being exchanged between the other three. "Thirty hours ago we were all in a wedding. Isn't this supposed to be a time for romance?" She grinned with mischief in her eyes.

"Mind your own business and we'll mind ours." Jennifer returned her grin. "Right now, your business is learning to surf and Jess is just the person to teach you."

"Really! I watched the surfing championships on TV and—"

"Hold it, young lady." Lee caught Katie's gaze.

"Nothing like the surfing championships for you. Only small waves and *not* on the North Shore."

Katie's brow wrinkled. "North Shore?"

"That's where the trade winds pile the surf up on the north end of Oahu. Twenty-foot waves are common. They can reach thirty feet or more." Lee lifted his hand high above his head for emphasis. "Tons of water crash down breaking boards, breaking bones, breaking…"

"I get it, Lee. No big waves. But they do sound like fun." She giggled.

A young man about twenty years old set glasses on the table in front of them. His eyes made frequent darting glances at Katie. After positioning the last glass, he stood up and faced her. "Pardon me, but I've got to ask. Are you the karate girl from the yacht, the one who's been on TV for the past two hours?"

Katie frowned. "What do you mean on TV?"

The musician had taken a break. The waiter walked to a TV mounted on the wall, turned it on, and flipped a few channels. Soon a video of the yacht exploding into flames lit the screen. The video clip was followed by pictures of Katie and Jennifer, pictures obviously borrowed from the Seattle media.

"That's what I mean," the young man said. "And those pictures don't do you two justice." He looked at Katie. "How long will you be on the island? I—"

"Hold it." Katie stood and met the waiter's gaze. "I think you need to know a few facts. Jennifer's married. She's my mom."

"Mom?" The young man looked puzzled.

"And I'm only fifteen."

"Fifteen? Excuse me. I didn't mean—"

Lee spoke. "Oh, yes you did. I can't say I blame

you though. But she *is* only fifteen. When she's old enough to spend time with guys, they have to come through me and Jenn." He nodded towards Jennifer. "And Granddad is a black belt in karate. Sixth degree."

Katie batted her eyelids at the young man. "As you can see, I'm fairly well protected."

"And as you can see, I'm fairly well embarrassed. But you are—"

"A knockout." Lee said. "Yeah. She can *do* that, too."

The waiter stepped backward. "That's what they said on the news. Uh, I'll be back for your order in a couple minutes."

Lee looked at Katie after she sat down. "That's twice. And how many times have you gone into restaurants since you arrived?"

Katie giggled. "Twice. Boys are silly, aren't they? "

Jennifer placed a hand on her shoulder. "So are men, sometimes." She paused. "Well, Katie and Granddad are going to Oahu to visit relatives. What about us?" She locked gazes with him.

"I've been thinking—"

"So have I. We only got to see that room on the water for a few minutes. Long enough to see how incredible the view of sunsets will be, and then we left for..." she stopped.

He took her hand. "We don't have to think about that anymore."

"Would they would let us have the room for a few more nights than we reserved? The room was—"

"I know. The room was special." Lee said. "I'll ask when we get there after dinner."

After dinner..." Katie looked at her great-grandfather. "Granddad, do you suppose they would let me see Anya?"

37

Katie stared through the car window. On her right were green sugarcane fields, on her left some kind of plantation. It would be wonderful if the future held an opportunity for her to live in the islands. The future..."Granddad, what do you think will happen to Anya? She's cooperating with all of the law enforcement organizations, but she *did* work with the traffickers. By coercion, but still..."

"I don't know what the authorities will decide to do with her. They will protect her until the trials, but after that...who knows? Her testimony at the trials could put her in danger with other international criminals."

"So she needs to be in the Witness Protection Program."

Granddad nodded. "You and I may think so. But as Lee and Agent Peterson said, the Department of Justice makes that determination. But you know what?"

"Questions." Katie smiled, glancing at her great granddad. "You're beginning to talk like Lee. Just say it."

He smiled and patted her hand. "If you tell Anya the good news you promised her, her future could turn out good no matter what the Department of Justice decides."

"You're right. I shouldn't be worrying about

anything except how to present a loving, heavenly Father to someone who has only been treated horribly by men."

"That's the crux of it." Granddad's gaze reached far down the road ahead. "There's Wailuku. Why don't you pray about it until we get there? Maybe God has some good ideas. After all, He is the One who created Anya. He knows her heart."

Katie glanced at the wise man sitting beside her in the car. He had committed his life to the Savior not even two days ago, yet he came up with answers which demonstrated a spiritual insight that amazed her. Regardless, he had given her an idea and she would go with it. Maybe Granddad was right. She slipped into silent prayer while the car rolled into the outskirts of Wailuku.

When a policewoman escorted Anya into the room, Katie noticed Anya was wearing street clothes. What did that mean? And why were they allowing them to meet with no glass wall between them. It was nothing like the prison visits she'd seen on TV.

Katie stood, extended her arms, and stepped towards the beautiful blonde.

Anya's puzzled expression softened to a weak smile, and she stepped into Katie's arms.

Katie gave her a hug, and then held her shoulders, pushing Anya back to study her face. "Are you doing OK?"

"Yeah. I think so. At least no one here is going to hurt me."

What would it be like to have that concern constantly on one's mind? Maybe like it was for Katie when she was tied up on the yacht and heard footsteps outside her cabin door. Always wondering, no certainty about her future.

Certainty about her future. *That's where I can help her.*

"Do you remember the good news I told you about?"

"I thought you were just trying to make me feel better. Trying to be nice." Anya's gaze dropped to the floor.

Katie gently raised Anya's chin until she could see her eyes. "Can you think of one reason I should be nice to you?"

Anya face tilted downward again. She frowned and dropped her shoulders. "You don't have any reasons to be—"

"That's not true, Anya."

"But you said you didn't have any reason to—"

"No. That's not what I said. I asked you to give me even one reason why I should be nice to you. I can think of a lot of reasons. But I wanted to know what you thought. "

"You said there were a lot of reasons. So *you* name one." Anya's set jaw and rigid posture reflected the challenge of her words.

"I'll do better than that." Katie paused. "First, I love you and care about you."

"How can you say that, Katie? Especially after—"

"Let me finish, please." Katie waited a moment.

Anya met her gaze.

Good. She was listening, not just waiting to interrupt. "I can say that because it's true. Also because my Lord and Savior, Jesus, told me to love you, to love everyone, even my enemies, so—"

"Is that what I am to you? Your enemy?"

"To be honest, right after you helped them take

me, I considered you my enemy. But not anymore."

"But, Katie." Anya's eyes grew wide, intense. "When you ran towards me at the house in Kihei, you were going to kill me."

"What you said then...well, I went a little bit crazy when I saw you. But I hoped you'd forgive me, because my Heavenly Father told me to love others like I love myself."

"Father? Father equals man. You can't trust them. They make you...serve them. God...He would be the same way."

Katie had anticipated Anya's resistance to anything male. But still...

Please, Lord, give me the words.

"This God, the only true God, does ask us to serve Him, but only if we trust Him and love Him."

"I don't love or trust the men I'm forced to serve. I couldn't do that."

"That's because they don't love *you*." Katie tried to give Anya her warmest smile. It was easy to smile because now she could tell her the good news. "God loves you with an infinite love, a love so deep and complete that He loves you just the way you are."

"And you really expect me to believe that? Katie, you know some of the things I've done."

"I don't expect you to believe without some proof. You see, I said He loves you like you are because, like me, you're not perfect."

"I didn't need you to tell me that, the men that—"

"Please, let me finish."

Anya pursed her lips and stood, studying Katie's face, waiting.

"God loves us and wants to have a close relationship with us but, like you agreed, we aren't perfect. But God is, and He won't have relationships with people who aren't."

"And this is your good news?" Anya rolled her eyes.

"Yeah. I know. It doesn't sound very good...yet. But if we somehow paid for our imperfections, then we *could* have a relationship with Him."

"What does that take? And what about the times we mess up in the future after that?"

Anya was smart. But best of all, she was thinking. She was into their discussion despite all her objections.

"The payment for our sins, Anya, is our death."

"Great! So after I die, I get to have a relationship with God?"

"Not exactly. The kind of death it takes to pay for sin, even one sin, is permanent death, separation from God for ever, infinite separation."

"I don't even know why I listened to you. You set me up, give me hope, and then spring this joke on me. You're cruel, Katie!"

Katie studied Anya's face. She didn't look angry, just hurt. Deeply hurt and betrayed. As bad as it sounded, it was another good sign. She had won Anya's confidence or there could have been no accusation of betrayal. But she would now have to win it again.

Please, Lord, it's time for You to do that thing You do to people's hearts.

Katie took a deep breath and met Anya's hostile gaze. The hurt she saw there reflected back, shredding her own heart. Katie's eyes filled with tears. When they overflowed, she wiped her cheek. "I do love you, Anya. God loves you too, and He proved it."

Katie waited.

No reply.

"The permanent death I told you about, God paid it Himself, using Jesus."

Anya was silent.

Katie waited for a response. Waited and prayed.

Slowly Anya's mouth opened, and she stared into Katie's eyes. Her eyes blazed with fire. "If I do this, I've got to know that this isn't some cruel joke. I don't want to be hurt by—" Anya's tears spilled onto her cheeks as she sobbed.

Katie wrapped her arms around Anya and held her as her body shook with emotion. She waited to see if Anya would tell her what was really on her heart.

Anya's sobbing had attracted attention.

A policewoman entered the room and stepped towards the two girls.

Katie saw Granddad's stern headshake. The woman backed off and slipped out the door.

After another minute, Anya's sobs subsided, but she left her head resting on Katie's shoulder. "I have to know…for sure, or I can't make a commitment like that."

Katie motioned for Granddad to come.

He stood and approached the girls.

"Granddad, my Bible is in my suitcase in the trunk of the car. If you get it for me, do you suppose they would let you come back in with it?"

"They may have Bibles here in the jail."

"No." Katie shook her head. "Anya needs *my* Bible, the special one that Jenn bought for me. It's marked up so she can find all the passages she needs to read."

The door opened and a man in a suit entered. "They told me you were here. I'm Detective Ramirez."

Granddad shook the detective's hand. "Sir, we have a somewhat unusual request. We need my granddaughter's Bible. It's in our car."

"I see…" The detective said as he rubbed his chin. "Come with me, Mr. Akihara, is it?"

"Yes, it is."

"I think I can help you."

After the two men left the room, Katie spoke softly. "There *is* proof, Anya. A lot of it. I have an apologetical Bible, a version for people who want proof. There's a book in it, kind of like a chapter, called the book of John. When you read it, think about what you're reading, about what the people did and why they did it. Ask God to show you the truth. You do that, and you'll have all the proof you need."

"So faith isn't just a blind thing?" Anya's voice was barely a whisper.

Katie shook her head. "After you read how they whipped those people, tortured, and killed many of them, people who lived at the time of Jesus, you tell me if you think their faith was blind." She paused to let the information sink in. "If theirs wasn't blind, and we have their historical record to read, ours doesn't have to be blind either."

Katie studied Anya's face. "You don't look entirely convinced. That's OK. Just promise me you'll read what I show you in my Bible. That's all I ask."

Anya smiled weakly. "I'll read it. It's the only place I have to turn to for hope right now."

Katie grinned at her. "You got that right, girl. It's the only place any of us have to turn to for hope."

After Granddad returned and gave Katie her Bible, she moved the ribbon marker to the book of John, handed the book to Anya, and turned to leave.

"Hey, Crazy Katie."

Katie turned around and Anya's arms wrapped around her in a tight embrace.

"Hey, Awesome Anya. See you…at the trials if not before. If you get a chance to call me, my phone number is inside the front cover."

Katie turned, knowing she would never forget the picture of Anya, her tear-streaked face looking down into an opened Bible.

38

Lee took Jennifer's hand as they turned from the security checkpoint at Kahului Airport and walked towards the exit nearest the temporary parking area. "With Katie and Granddad boarding for Oahu, what would you like to do, Jenn?"

She met his gaze and gave him a smile which ended in a display of glowing, pink cheeks.

He looked at her face and squeezed her hand. "That sounds like a wonderful idea."

She poked his shoulder and leaned her cheek against the spot where she'd unleashed her mock fury.

"At least I got better treatment than you gave that guy called Snake—"

"Stop it, Lee. That's history. History I don't even want to think about right now. Let's focus on the future, our future."

Her coy smile and warm, inviting eyes derailed his train of thought.

"Our future. Let's see. If we save enough, we can easily retire at fifty-five and—"

She poked him again.

"Okay. I get it...the *near-term* future." He unlocked the car with the key fob and grinned.

She did not. "Lee, let's get in our car, *now*, and drive straight to our room."

"My sentiments ex—" The trade winds swirled through the parked cars around them and sent

Jennifer's thick, dark hair dancing. Was it a waltz or tango? Regardless, it gave him an idea. "As we drive out by the rental lots, I'm going to exchange our car for a convertible."

His words drew a headshake. "It would only mess up my hair…and waste time."

"But you look very, very sexy with your hair a little windblown." He opened the door for her.

"I can read your eyes, Lee. I've always been able to. You thought I looked, you know, since that night we met."

"Guilty as charged." Lee climbed in and started the car. Before driving out of the lot he scanned golden landscape and the sky with several layers of scattered clouds. "Things are shaping up for a wonderful sunset tonight. Beginning in about thirty minutes. We need to hurry."

"Just don't get us into an accident. And no traffic tickets, either. No delays." She rested a hand on his shoulder.

Fifteen minutes later they were westbound on Highway 311 towards Kihei in a silver convertible, rolling along at forty-five miles per hour with the top down. Jennifer's hair waved gently in the breeze. He looked longingly at it. "See. I told you so."

"Keep your eyes on the road, Mr. Brandt." She paused. "You enjoy teasing me, embarrassing me. Why do I put up with you?"

"Because about thirty hours ago you promised you would for as long as we—"

"Yes. But if you don't keep your eyes on the road, I might be prematurely released from my promise."

"That's not going to happen. Not after I finally found someone I love, someone I can give my heart to and trust not to trash it. Someone who happens to be a consensus Miss Universe, and—"

"That's what one of the men on the yacht called me. No more Miss Universe talk, please."

"How about Mrs. Brandt?"

She loosened her seatbelt, leaned over the console and against his shoulder. "Much better, sweetheart. Much, much better."

Lee slowed the car and turned from North Kihei Road onto the long driveway of the resort. "Did you like our room?"

Jennifer let out a long, slow sigh. "Yes. I only got to see it for a few minutes, but the room was wonderful. You know, that seems so long ago that—"

"Almost a lifetime ago?" He gave her his mischievous smile.

"Almost a lifetime? Don't joke about it, Lee." Jennifer gave him a frown and a pleading look. "Can we please talk about something more pleasant?"

"Sure. I've got an idea that just might work to make things very pleasant."

"What idea?"

"Let me surprise you."

She snuggled her head deeper into his shoulder. "I'm sure there will be a lot of surprises tonight."

"Amen for surprises."

"C'mon, Lee. You're supposed to be talking softly, saying sweet, romantic things. Maybe even a little...suggestive."

"How would I know that? I've never done this before. But I thought I nailed the suggestive part."

"Sometimes, Lee Brandt, I could kill you."

"I haven't heard *that* in a while. You used to say it all the time." He stopped the car in the parking lot.

"That's because lately I've preferred this." Jennifer pulled him into a soft, sweet, enticing kiss. "Now let's get the matter of the room settled because this is our wedding night."

He opened the door. "Yeah, let's do that. I didn't particularly care for the dress rehearsal."

"Only pleasant things, remember?" Jennifer said as they walked towards the registration desk.

He took Jennifer's hand when they approached the young man working the counter. "Hi, I'm Lee Brandt and this is—"

"I know who *you* are. Excuse me, please. I'll just be a second." He turned towards an office behind the counter. "They're here, sir."

An older Hawaiian gentleman emerged from the office. He studied their faces and smiled. "Lee and Jennifer Brandt, I'm glad to meet you. I'm the manager here. We are so sorry you had such a terrible experience, but so thankful you're all right. Everyone involved in tourism on the island is indebted to you for putting an end to that horrible organization. Besides that, if tourists are being abducted by human traffickers on Maui, it would be economically disastrous to us." He chuckled. "Worse than the runway revision at the airport, and that's costing us a cool half-billion dollars in tourist trade."

Lee met the gentleman's gaze. "Frankly, sir, we're just glad to be alive and to finally begin the honeymoon we intended to start yesterday."

"I know you didn't get to spend the night there, but how do you like the room?"

"We love it," Jennifer said, stepping close to Lee's side. "You can hear the waves lapping right under the window. It's...it's perfect."

The manager rubbed his hands briskly together. "That's wonderful." He focused on Lee. "How long are you staying on the island?"

"Three weeks," Lee said. "We were supposed to move to a condo in Wailea tomorrow."

The manager looked from Lee to Jennifer. "Would you like to have the room for three weeks?"

Jennifer gasped and looked at Lee. "We'd love it."

"How much would it cost," Lee added.

"Your room was broken into before you arrived, then after the events of last night and today—the room is free. It's on us. Actually, all of the major hotels on the island agreed on this shortly after the news reported you two were all right." He pursed his lips and stood waiting.

Lee frowned. "But doesn't someone else have it reserved for at least part of the three weeks?"

"I'll make them an offer they can't refuse." The manager grinned. "They'll take it, and be glad to do it."

Lee looked at Jennifer's smile, the pleading look in her eyes, and shrugged back at the manager. "Thanks. We accept your kind offer."

"Good. Gary here will get you registered for your three week stay. Enjoy the room. Aloha."

The young man stepped up to the counter holding some already prepared forms. He laid the forms on the counter and focused on Jennifer. "So you were on the yacht that blew up?"

She gave him a tightlipped smile. "I was. But I escaped quite a while before the explosion."

"We heard those guys were international criminals. Ma'am, would you mind telling me how you escaped?"

Jennifer sighed. "My granddad is a sixth degree

black belt in karate. He taught me well." She paused. "However, our daughter was on the yacht seconds before it exploded."

The clerk scanned Jennifer and cocked his head. "Your daughter?" You mean they had a toddler on that yacht?"

"She escaped, too."

"Did that blonde babe help your daughter escape?"

"The blonde babe *is* our daughter."

"But you're—"

"Older than I look." Jennifer gave him another tightlipped smile. "And Katie is younger than she looks. She's fifteen. We're adopting Katie."

Jennifer stepped up to the counter. "Where do we sign? Lee, I would like to go now, please."

Lee put a hand on her shoulder. "You don't want me to get us iced lattes first?" He signed the forms while Jennifer glared at him.

When they turned to leave she took his hand. "That wasn't funny, Lee. For the next three weeks, I'm not letting you out of my sight for any reason."

"Jenn, just before you disappeared, do you know what I was thinking?"

"With a guy who grew up hunting and fishing around Iron Mountain, crawling into flea-infested caves, driving at night without his headlights, one who teaches fifteen-year-old girls how to shoot AK-47s, who knows?"

He pulled her close. "Weren't we going to forget the bad history? When you were looking into that jewelry case, I was thinking I'd never seen any woman anywhere as beautiful as you."

"Look at me. I just spent the night tied up,

drugged, and then swam five hundred yards through salt water. I haven't had a shower. My hair is stringy and salty and I—"

He stopped her diatribe with his lips. After their kiss, he held her close and spoke softly. "Right now, just the way you are, I could stand you next to any woman on the planet, and every man would agree with me. I don't know how or why God gave me someone like you. I'm just an ordinary—"

She pressed her hand over his lips. Jennifer's heart ached from Lee's words. How could someone as wonderful as Lee think he was ordinary, somehow not worthy of her? She was the one with a bad temper, the unforgiving one, the one who had trouble trusting God. "Stop it, Lee Brandt. There's nothing ordinary about you. From the way you think to how you've risked your life for mine. In you God gave me the man I needed to lead me to Him, to be my partner in life, to be my husband." She pressed her cheek into his chest listening to his heartbeat. The rhythm of her life. "I think it's time to go to our room now, before anything else happens."

"Before anything else happens? It's not like we might—"

"Yes, it is. Knowing you is dangerous. Do you realize since I met you I've been chased and shot at by terrorists, chased and shot at by human traffickers, nearly drowned in a flooding river, washed off the beach in a storm surge, captured to be sold into slavery twice, and chased by Iranian undercover agents who had some really bad plans for me, all this in only nine months? Am I going to survive this marriage?"

"It's not fair to blame me for all that. You've put a little spin on things. The story needs to be put into perspective."

"Perspective? I'll give you perspective. I was terrified over and over again. What perspective can you give that's going to change all that?"

"You." He slowly scanned her face and continued down her body to her feet. "The perspective is you. The terrorists and Iranians wanted you because of your mind. The traffickers wanted you...well, for all the rest. The storm surge nearly got you because of your pigheaded stubbornness. It all happened because of you, not me. Let's face it, you need me, Jenn, to protect you from yourself."

Her eyes burned through him like lasers. "Of all the arrogant—"

Lee's growing, coy smile stopped her words, but not all the feelings boiling inside.

He put his hands on her shoulders. They were warm, strong, and inviting, but she wasn't going to step into his arms. Not yet.

She met his gaze. Like his hands, his eyes were also warm and inviting, unlike his words a few seconds ago. He was teasing her, probably like he did his younger brother and sister growing up. Teasing was part of who he was.

He continued. "I need you...for life...for love...for..."

She didn't hear the rest. She was in his arms, wondering why she started the stupid, distracting conversation.

You're an idiot with a 200 IQ, Jennifer Brandt. And that's the worst kind.

"Lee," she whispered, "it's time to go to our room. Let's leave the car here and walk down. By the way, what was the secret idea you wouldn't tell me?"

"I don't have to tell you. The guy at the hotel did it for me."

"Do you mean you were going to try to get the room for the rest of our time here, and you didn't even ask me?" She gave him her mock frown.

"I asked you if you liked the room."

She smiled knowingly. "Yes, you did."

When they reached the door, Lee unlocked it and scooped her off her feet. He draped her across his arms, and carried her into the room.

"You already did this once, remember?"

"We're starting fresh tonight. A complete do-over, remember? After all, *this* is our wedding night and I want it to be perfect." He stood her on her feet and took her hand. "Come on, Jenn."

He tugged gently on her hand, and she followed him up the stairs.

When they stepped into the loft bedroom, Jennifer stopped. They hadn't gotten this far yesterday. As she studied the room, a smile spread across her face.

This was a '60s resort which hadn't had a facelift in thirty years. Regardless, this room was special. It was open to the air, with screens at the east and west ends. The trade winds, slowed by the surrounding trees, passed through creating a gentle, refreshing flow of air.

The large window on the beach side looked out across Maalaea Bay. In the distance, at the south end of Lanai, the sun was a brilliant red ball, nearly on the horizon. Waves splashed gently below the window, creating an atmosphere that combined the sensations of sight, sound, temperature, and humidity in ways no one could possibly imagine by looking at the old building from the outside. Palm fronds waved gently in the breeze at the top of the picture window.

Her gaze moved back to the red sun. It painted the lowest clouds various shades of yellow and orange, while above them the higher clouds remained tufts and striations of white painted on a deep-blue, tropical sky.

She backed up to the end of the bed and sat down staring out the window at the sunset. "This is absolutely beautiful, Lee."

He looked towards the setting sun for a few seconds and gave her his warmest smile, then pointed upward, out the window. "Tell me about the clouds. What do you see?"

Our wedding night and he's giving me a quiz on Meteorology 101. "There are cumulus clouds hugging the hills. Patches of altocu above that and, let's see…some wispy cirrus at about thirty thousand feet."

"More like forty thousand feet."

"But, Lee, sunset in the tropics is sixty seconds of blazing glory, and then nighttime."

He shook his head. "Just watch. Tonight this will go on for at least forty minutes. The sun has clouds to light up all the way to forty thousand feet."

He sat down beside her and slipped his arm around her waist. "This is why I pulled you up the stairs. When we came in, it was just beginning."

Her gaze was glued to the sunset beyond the big window. "I wouldn't have believed you even if you tried to describe this to me."

"There's no way you can describe this. Not with words. God painted it, and He gave us eyes to see it. All we can do is sit here and enjoy it."

She smiled warmly at him. "For now, that's enough, sweetheart."

"For now?"

"Yes, for now. Let's just watch the sunset unfold. Every few seconds the colors change. Look, Lee, the second layer of clouds is turning from white to golden."

"Am I forgiven for my secret plans about the room?"

"I think so."

He pulled his head back. "What do you mean, you *think* so?"

"To everything there is a season. A time to forgive, a time to talk, and a time to just look and enjoy...and a time for love. Let me give you a hint. This isn't the time for talking."

"I see."

She leaned her head on his shoulder. "Now you've got it, sweetheart."

He pulled her head close, kissed her forehead, and they watched the cirrus at forty thousand feet begin to show color.

Thirty minutes later, she sat by Lee's side on the foot of the bed and watched the highest clouds turn from crimson to pink and gray, against a cobalt-blue sky. A bright silver moon hung over Maalaea Bay. The green palm fronds in the big window had become dark silhouettes waving gently to them, inviting them to enjoy the evening. Waves splashed below the window and their soothing melody filled the room with tropical delight. Even the humidity added to the delightful, sensual feeling.

Lee turned and looked into her eyes. "It was spectacular." He sighed. "But it's ending."

She looked into his eyes and saw enough love to fill a lifetime. "Lee, I shouldn't have to prompt you. This is the part where you kiss me and—"

He pulled her close, to that place of security against his beating heart. Their time had finally come.

When his lips joined hers, she melted into his kiss like the chocolate truffles she often stirred into her steaming hot lattes. The milk and chocolate swirled together until they became one, producing a rich, sweet, delightful drink she could never tire of. Like their life together...which was only beginning.

Author's Notes:

Maui was a wonderful place to send my first main characters, Jennifer and Lee, for their honeymoon. But with its gentle waves, warm sun, a surfeit of sandy beaches, spectacular sunsets, warm water teeming with colorful fish begging me to slip on my snorkel and mask, and people wagging the hang-loose sign if I get too uptight, how could I possibly set a thriller on Maui? Since I'm not into man-eating sharks, there's only one way. You have to import the bad guys. When I was done with them, I had to deport the criminals, either to crypts or to the cooler.

If you haven't guessed by now, the setting of this third book in the series is my favorite vacation spot. Since 2008, my wife, Babe, and I have been blessed with opportunities to spend more than 14 weeks on Maui. We've taken more than 18 GB of digital images, including panoramic shots of all our favorite beaches on the island.

Knowing the island well minimized the research for this book, and it permitted me to adapt the story to the setting. I only had to modify a few small things to accommodate the story. So, in *Moon over Maalaea Bay*, you get Maui like it really is…well, after you subtract the bad guys. For example, the sunset description at the end of the book was borrowed from the most beautiful sunset I have ever seen, one that Babe, and I watched and photographed in 2010 from Keawakapu Beach in Kihei.

I hope you have enjoyed the series about the geniuses, Jennifer and Lee, and their foster daughter, Katie. You'll probably see them again soon in another story.

Acknowledgments

Many thanks to my critique group, Dawn Lilly and Gayla Hiss, for steering me towards a much better start and ending to this story. I forgive both of you for making me throw away the first 10,000 words. Thanks once again to my wife, Babe, for her willingness to listen to the story countless times and for giving me time to write when my pen was hot, even when she had other plans for us. Finally, thanks to my editor, Jamie West, for catching the logical and emotional holes in my story and for teaching me more about writing from my female protagonist's point of view.

Thank you for purchasing this Harbourlight title. For other inspirational stories, please visit our on-line bookstore at www.pelicanbookgroup.com.

For questions or more information, contact us at customer@pelicanbookgroup.com.

Harbourlight Books
The Beacon in Christian Fiction™
an imprint of Pelican Ventures Book Group
www.pelicanbookgroup.com

May God's glory shine through
this inspirational work of fiction.

AMDG

www.ingramcontent.com/pod-product-compliance
Lightning Source LLC
Chambersburg PA
CBHW051240250626
47155CB00009B/3111